Ac

A Bettei

"Hard hitting stories of lives o.. ... .i > cuge.
    —Paul D. Brazill, author of *Too Many Crooks*
      A Case of Noir and *Guns of Brixton*

"Beau Johnson is a lawless writer. His renegade cop Bishop Rider, a battered and bruised, world-weary hero forced to operate outside a corrupt system to find justice. And that's what these stories have in common: justice, in all its muted, corrupt glory. Johnson operates in shades of gray, where sometimes all it takes is for a bad man to kill a worse one. A stark and sobering reality, and a stellar debut."
    —Joe Clifford, author of
    the Jay Porter Thriller Series

"Beau's ability to strike at the heart of human emotion is both unnerving, uncanny, and unique. It allows him to wring tears from the darkest recesses of the human experience. A dark chameleon who slides from twisted villain to damaged innocent like a well-tuned master of fiction. A how-to on the craft of short fiction."
    —Tom Pitts, author of *Hustle* and *American Static*

"An uneasy collection, Johnson crafts each story with masterful precision and an icy cold edge. Dripping with psychological terror, nerve racking suspense and characters unhinged, *A Better Kind of Hate* is an offering of patience, plans, and revenge. Johnson's talent is spectacular and terrifying."
    —Marietta Miles, author of *Route 12*

"Beau Johnson writes from that place inside us all that is nothing but brutal honesty and grit. And while most people avoid this place, Beau milks it for every word he can."
    —Ryan Sayles, author of
    the Richard Dean Buckner series

A BETTER
KIND OF HATE

BEAU JOHNSON

A BETTER KIND OF HATE

STORIES

DOWN&OUT
BOOKS

Down & Out Books
3959 Van Dyke Rd, Ste. 265
Lutz, FL 33558
www.DownAndOutBooks.com

The characters and events in this book are fictitious. Any similarity to real persons, living or dead, is coincidental and not intended by the author.

Cover design by Eric Beetner

ISBN: 1-943402-92-2
ISBN-13: 978-1-943402-92-2

For my parents
The ones who survived
and the one who did not

CONTENTS

FIRE IN THE HOLE

I push the steel harder into the back of Terrance's shaved head.

"C'mon," he says. "You and me, Rider, we've similar goals." The scum was right as well as wrong. Where I saw him and his kind as a means to an end, he only wanted atop the pile. "We're businessmen, you and I. Way I see it, the info I'm givin' you, I should be gettin' a free pass."

"Anne-Marie Shields. Did she get a pass?" Terrance was smart, played dumb, but I already knew. Put a bullet in his crotch to make him understand. I unloaded the remaining five just to let off steam.

"And this piece of shit, this Terrance, he said Toomey and his men are coming in night after next?" Batista continued to look out over Culver, the city he'd sworn to protect. Duty and honor are the things which make up Detective John Batista; what made up most of the men he stood in line with. That he now found himself in my world was something we rarely discussed. It was a given, what I did. And he'd yet to try and turn me in.

In him I see myself, a time when belief had been the

norm; that this world did in fact not kick at its dead. Detective Batista and I, we have our demons, sure, each the thing that drives us on. But to be fair, that is where the similarities end. No matter how much he might think otherwise.

Toomey, though…Toomey was the here and now. And Toomey was trouble. Aggressive. Ruthless. Feral. He was high-end too, lacking the moral compass most considered a conscience. Word on the street was he kept a portable wood chipper now, and that the man was unafraid to take his time if given the chance.

Bangers wouldn't use him, slingers either, which left me two choices, both of which I could work with. Russians or Italians. Little more recon and Bobby Carmine popped into view.

"Head-shit looking to take you out, I see." Batista runs a hand through his greying hair, goes down about his goatee and finishes with a sigh. Politics notwithstanding, I swear the man's as textbook as they come.

"What it looks like, yeah."

"And just what is it you want from me?" I looked to the city's lights behind him, looked down into the valley which had claimed so many. Culver was not the place I'd been born, but I was certain it'd be the place I'd die.

"I want unobstructed access to the south side when this goes down. I'm not looking for collateral damage. Ensure the night's patrol is light."

He looks at me, shakes his head, and then says he'd work on it: Batista-speak for yes.

"You're going to need ordnance, then." I told him yes, but that it wouldn't be coming from him. As ever, he'd already done more than enough.

Outside Carmine's place I load the launcher as soon as I see that Toomey and his crew are given the go-through. Ten minutes later and I light the night. Upon entering, I can't help but think back to men like Toomey. Hell, to men like Carmine himself. Lowlifes who think they deserve; men arrogant enough to believe the streets were theirs; who would rob and kill and extort and have others do the very same thing in their name. I picture Mick the Fish, Danny Dolan, and Marcel Abrum. They were special, each of them, all receiving a little extra piece of my time. To Toomey I would do the same. He of the wood chipper fame deserved no less.

As the Kevlar takes two to the chest I turn, dive, but take one in the side of the leg as I return fire. I hear a click. Another. And then the gun as it's tossed aside.

"Come if yer comin' goddammit!" I did. It was Toomey, of course. Why men like him never died like the rest of them I will never know for sure.

Through the debris and flame and smoke I see what he's become—intestines that stream outwards, flowing in place of his legs. Thick, they wind around brick and plaster like pregnant string. He gurgles, spits up, and as I approach I step on as much of him as I can. In the end I don't need bullets. I only look him in the eye.

To protect and serve, Batista says. To protect and save, I respond.

I admit the difference is vast.

FRONT, THEN CENTER

Not one of them, but two, and it'd been narrowed down to Sacks and Jimmy D. Both were tall, both were built, and both held their faces as men like them should; that they would not take shit from anyone, not unless I told them to.

Each was fucking my wife.

Where Jimmy D was white, Anton Sacks was black. I say this to prove differences; that I am a man who clearly sees. Not as one might think, but as one who has proven his ability to adapt and survive in an industry which will always be less than kind.

"You want I should pull the car around, Boss?"

I look up to the big man. His suit is tight, his hair tighter, and all at once I picture him taking Miranda from behind. This isn't the first time something like this has occurred. Moreover, it's that I hate admitting as much, as admission is akin to weakness, especially when respect is involved. My father taught me this, usually doing so with his fists. Same as the smell of his after-shave, I have remembered such lessons well. *You mess with the bull; you get the horns* being first front, then center.

"Yeah, Sacksy, you go get the car. Be nice to end it early for a night." It's then that I turn my attention toward my number two, my Jimmy D. His entire dick is wedged within Miranda's young, sweet mouth, her entire throat engorged. I know it's not real, not really-real before my eyes, but I know it's happened regardless, there behind my back. How do I know this? I pay people. How the fuck else? Another sage piece of advice courtesy of a man I'd come to hate.

"Not really much to look at tonight anyway, eh, Boss?" He was right, the talent up on stage far from the best we'd employed. I make a mental note to do something about that—once this current set of circumstances had been remedied, of course.

And that each of them still called me Boss, every day, even though they continued to ball what wasn't theirs—that's what chafed me most, I suppose. Made a man angrier than he has any right being, taxing his emotional limits past a point he'd ever want to see. This is all conjecture, of course, so one need not get their panties in a bunch. The old rules still played here, same as they ever did.

"I ever tell you about that time my father took me to task for stealing lunch money in grade school?" Jimmy's expression is counter to the one I pay him to provide, looking less than thrilled that I began what I had and more like he wished he were someplace else. Made me smile is what this did, but not for the reasons you might think. "No, Boss, I can't rightly recall you doing so."

Can't rightly recall? Really? Fine. We'd play it this way then.

To Jimmy it was just another day in the life, another dollar, so he doesn't sense anything when I tell him I want a moment alone with Bruce. Once Bruce is beside me I give him the man his cue. Ten minutes later I have what I want: the place is a ghost, the music is gone, and the house lights are up. During this time Sacks had come back in, the car brought round, and takes his usual place three feet behind wherever I am.

Contrary to what people believe, there is an I in team.

My old man again, rearing his head as he's always done. I used the phrase anyway, stating it as I tell them to take their seats, saying we had some business to discuss. To his credit, I sense that Sacks recognizes that something is off, but still, he does nothing but what I ask of him. It's only when Bruce walks onto the stage with his wheelbarrow that we come to the bones of it. I especially appreciated how he'd arranged her head, there atop her thighs, almost as if he'd taken the time and done the hair himself. The way it was matted there, tucked behind the ears, tufts of blonde gold curving toward red.

From behind we are joined by a couple more of my guys, Gus and Frankie P. They come slowly, guns drawn, and take the two pieces Jimmy D and Sacks wished they were holding. I don't know this for fact, but it's the very thing I'd want if our roles had been reversed. Last but not least are the two bull queers I'd purchased just that morning. One black, one white, they come in naked except for their G-strings. Like it should, it adds an air of symmetry to the proceedings, and if I'm anything, it's a man who loved his symmetry.

"So the story I was wanting to tell is of the time I took a thing that didn't belong to me." They are not stupid men, not in every regard, and their faces begin to release everything I'd hoped for. This should have relieved me, but no, the images continued to come—these two men I'd employed for years now double-teaming the woman who'd given me my son, one deep into her snatch by way of his tongue and the other at home where the sun didn't shine. "It reminds me of this kid I once knew, we'll call him Billy. Billy was a scrawny little fuck with sticks for bones. Whenever we'd come to teams, it wasn't that he was picked last, but that he wasn't picked at all. Shit like that leaves a certain kind of scar on a person, creates a different type of rage. You see what I'm saying here?"

They did. I know they did. But it was only Jimmy D who spoke. "Way I see it, Boss, if you'd been able to satisfy your wife, well, she wouldn't have needed Sacksy or me at all. That much is obvious. But since she did, well, maybe a part of that lands on you. Whether you see this or not, I can't say. What I can pass on is this: she was the sweetest piece I ever took a run at, Boss. I mean, the throat on that woman. Damn." Not stupid, not in every regard, but I wasn't about to be baited, not after all the thought I'd put into this. And thus the scene was set, and suddenly I didn't care anymore—suddenly more angry with myself than anything.

It's a poor man who blames his instrument.

Really, Dad? Really?

But I was through with being polite. You fuck with something of mine I will fuck with something of yours. They knew that; had enforced the very rule. That's what gets me most of all—that despite knowing what I might do, they chose to continue anyway. The only consolation I receive is what I need: their screams. The ones that come as the two bull queers start giving them the horn.

More than the manner which ends them, it's this I will cherish most.

RIGHT TIME, RIGHT PLACE

Geared up, I meet Batista at the usual spot. The detective is thinner now, and his face is drawn. Behind the lines I see everything I need to; everything the both of us have sworn to correct.

"I've found him," I say and move forward, my eye line out toward Culver and down. The detective and I have been here many times before, this meeting place now ritual I suppose. It didn't change the fact that we were acknowledging the evil awaiting us below. If anything, it reinforced what we'd come to be about.

"Who?" And then it clicked; a pause as Batista goes and makes the leap. "Him? You're telling me Abrum's the guy?" I tell him more, plenty, how Marcel Abrum seemed to be the one who initiated it all. Batista voices his concern, cautions we can only take the information we received so far. I disagreed, telling him as much, stating that this was it, there was no turning back, after all this time we had finally found the truth.

Batista takes a moment, a hand up and through what remained of his hair. He then jams his hands into the pockets of his overcoat. Taking himself from the view of the lights below and the darkness beyond, he says:

"What the fuck are we waiting for then?"

He didn't need me to answer. Neither of us did.

Marcel Abrum took the spot left wide by Mick the Fish. Word on the street was he brought Toomey into the fray as well, back in the day. Toomey was vicious, feral, but broken down nothing more than a gun for hire. But one who housed a particular skill set; piece of shit bringing along a portable wood chipper wherever he could. Man was unafraid to use the machine either, not when given the time. I'd taken him and his crew out long ago, doing so with a launcher from inside a hundred yards. Through the fire and debris the man had somehow survived, his guts around him like snakes. I did what any sane man would, stepping on everything of him that remained, the world in turn becoming a much better place. But Marcel Abrum had been the man behind the man. And now I find out he had always been the man, from day one, since April and my mother went missing. It filled me with something larger than dread, burned with a heat you can only call hate. Not because I didn't know. But because I should have. The man had fingers in everything, all of it, the self-proclaimed Boss of Culver City since he took it from Mick the Fish. Was I blind? Too busy feeding my hate with low level scum to see the big guy for the trees? It would appear so.

Change was coming though. And with it, blood.

* * *

"I'll take the back," Batista says, and I nod. We both have the Kevlar on, each of us a helmet. If we were going to do it tonight, I told him we'd be doing it right. He laughed at that, a sour little thing, but I was used to his responses, even before he began losing the weight. "You say that like you give a shit. Like the both of us haven't been using each other this whole damn time." We're far from the same, Batista and I, but closer in our thinking now than in the past. This took some doing, and the time we found the cameras and cages had become the tipping point. Me, I've always hated scum; would eat it on a daily basis if given the chance. I had to be smart though, learning this long ago, and only because there was so much more to do.

April and my mother deserved no less.

Inside the strip club was a whole other story. Whatever had been going on, we had stepped into the middle of it.

I should have known though—the parking lot a ghost town except for a couple of SUVs. Once inside it's all screams and *oh my God make it stop*! When I round the corner I see why. Seems school was in session for a couple of guys who worked for Abrum—what I took from the set up anyway. Each man was naked from the waist down and bent over a table which Abrum sat in front of. From behind, each man was taking in another man, but not of their own accord. Two blacks, two whites, each on the other, like backwards symmetry. Around this stood other men, sentries in suits, hardware set firmly in hand. I counted five in total, along with the four entwined in whatever dance I'd walked into, this made nine.

I could deal with nine.

It was the look on Abrum's face I was having a hard time reconciling. It shouldn't have surprised me though, not this far down the rabbit hole.

I take the sentries out first, each to the head. Done, I move forward and all at once the men doing the raping are out of their victims and their hands are in the air. It doesn't stop what comes next, only slows each bullet down. The smell of what I'm doing is strong by now, but comforting, matching the strength I used to receive from believing in the soul.

"You about done?" And still he has yet move. He was watching me, yes, and with his hands out flat upon the table in front of him, but that was all. I'd be lying if I said I didn't find this peculiar.

Forward again, closer now, coming up behind the men who had been on the receiving end of the business going down before I arrived. They are wheezing, crying, with long strings of saliva hanging from their gobs. I make it quick, ending their misery, and then look Abrum in the eye. He's dressed to the nines, cufflinks and all, the handkerchief in his pocket a darker shade of blue than the million dollar suit.

"I want you to know it was never personal, Rider. This business, it demands the breaking of small cunts is all. It's this and nothing more."

I stand there, shocked, and a second too late I put it together. But by then Abrum had unloaded on me, and then I only saw dark.

"Was only a matter of time," I was on my back, an elephant on my chest. The shotgun was in Abrum's hand by now, the one which ripped through the bottom of the table and almost through the Kevlar. "I had to take precautions though, figuring a situation like this could very well take place. And you can't blame me, not after everything you've put down. I mean, you are a pit bull, Rider. You just do not let go." He was right, wise enough to realize as much, but still it would not help him, not once Batista made his move. This only worked if Batista was still alive, however, but even so, I'd survived worse.

"But being tonight of all nights, that is something. I mean, what I was doing here, explaining to the boys," He sweeps his hand around the room, kicking the two dead men closest to him. "I was trying to teach them what it was to take something from a man. Something that does not belong to them. They should have learned such things long ago, but people, they tend to sometimes forget. Not me though, Rider. Not when it comes to things concerning you."

The man had selective recall, or just liked to hear the sound of his own voice. I told him as much, but it didn't matter, not as it should. Once men like Abrum become accustomed to power they do not see the world as others do. No, it's then that reflection comes into play and the distortion which remains becomes the only focus, the only goal, and fuck every last person who gets in their way.

"Seeing where we're at, I can't see that making a difference, can you?" He bends down to me then, the oil in his hair glistening in the overhead light. His eyes are as I thought they'd be, beady and black, like pebbles dipped in tar. The elephant on my chest has been replaced by a rhinoceros, but at least I was getting more air. Around me blood pooled and flowed, the smell of copper trying its best to overtake what was already in the air. I tried to move, to sit up, but Abrum was on me before I got even halfway there.

"I don't think so," he says and stomps on my face not once but twice. My nose shatters and I think I feel my cheek bone break in two. They're good hits, clean, and stars come out to play as my head becomes cousins with the floor. I want to call out to Batista, I do, as he should have been there by now, but my mouth won't work, not how I liked. It meant one of two things. One was that my jaw had been broken as well. The other being Batista had been removed from the board. It's only when I think this does a third alternative come to mind. I shake it off, admonishing myself, but that's when it happens, when Batista steps from the shadows. For a moment I believe I'm wrong, the detective's face saying it all, but then he fires twice, each bullet into the man we'd come to stop. Abrum goes down hard, screaming, the broken bone and torn flesh of his knees meeting the ground with a sound I would come to dream of.

I shut my eyes: Checkmate, fucker.

"You need help up?" I did, and took Batista's outstretched arm. The rhinoceros was still on my chest but he was smaller now, half his former self. Abrum had moved from his knees to his side, the man semi-rolling in his pain. What came next was something that had been building for years.

Batista picks the man up and in front of a gold plated pole places him on the edge of the stage. Behind this pole sits a wheel barrel full of a woman's dismembered remains. We'd interrupted something for sure, that much was clear. We could never be the end of such things, no, and we'd be foolish to ever think along these types of lines. We could only continue as we were, for as long as we were able. It's a good lie. Brought on by how I picture them still. Not as they were, but how they'd been left.

"My sister was something you are not, the opposite in fact, but I want to say it regardless. I want you to have known." Duct tape next, up and around the man's hands, down and around his shattered knees. Done, Batista cuts through this tape as he cuts through Abrum. It brings pleading into the air, bribery, but mostly it was his flesh we coveted, his life. Fair trade I told him, not only for my family but all the people his existence had destroyed.

Surgery complete, Batista does what Batista has gotten better at: places pieces of Abrum into the afore-mentioned wheel barrel until it begins to overflow. "I'm going to assume this was a girlfriend of his. Maybe his wife. Either way, I'm sure she'd approve." I give Batista a grunt, and then start to work on my jaw. Takes some doing but in time I get it into a position I can manage. My nose is another issue entirely; same for the cheek. They'd heal. Abrum, however, would not.

On the whole, not a bad start to the week.

DICKS AND JARS AND A THIRD WORLD WAR

I needed to change the way I approached things. The laziness inherent to me is what prevented this from happening earlier I think, or maybe I'm wrong and it only comes down to what most of my life came down to: fear. Fear of failure. Fear of dying. Fear of sucking cock when I know I'm not meant to. This last one is what it's really about, the one which screamed loudest I suppose, but the admission of failure comes in at a hard second best. It was the dick sucking though, this what ate at me most. And just so we're clear, I'm not gay, not in the slightest, but certain things tend to occur once you make your way to prison, most of them being what you already know. It's different when you have to perform however, and goddamn if that ain't the truth. Does things to a man who isn't right with what's going down, making him a bigger target if he chooses to go and buck the program placed before him. Lucky for me I'm a fast learner.

Why was I like this? Fuck, who knows? I could say no mother or father but that'd be me making shit up. My life is what it is, and all I can do now is push forward and acknowledge my attempt at change. A planner now, everything I do is put down to paper and everything on it is then scoped out. No more cash and grabs for me. No more going in on a wing and a prayer. Two little things need to happen before I fully embrace this new way of life. It means facing certain fears already stated, sure, and only because the man instrumental to the big one is released just last week. Vic Sessions. Head queer of cellblock nine.

The man who made me his bitch.

Vic was actually Big Vic and he was larger than most of the men on the inside, in muscle as well as meat; my backside as tender today as that very first day, especially if the chair I choose is mostly made of wood. "You been duckin' me, I know." Eating at the worst type of mean he was the kind of bull queer who liked his eyeliner thick and his mustache thicker. The first time he and his boys come looking they find me in the laundry. I wasn't alone. Not then. But the silence their presence brings causes that to change, the place clearing out faster than fat kids to cherry cola. After that it's the cold steel of a big industrial trying to take an imprint of my face. Done, it's a sea of orange above me, and then a happy ending for all. "Not bad, Hollister. Not bad at all. Thing is, we're still gonna have to do something about them teeth." Monstrous. Evil. Prison-issued leather a taste no man would ever think to acquire.

Shit was enough to drive even the most well-adjusted straight man insane.

Vic wasn't done with me, though. Not for another nine months, three days, and as many goddamn hours. Only then was I reborn.

Reborn by way of freedom—time served in lieu of good behavior. Vic doesn't miss a beat at this, ensuring the honeymoon stage of our relationship is resurrected the night before I'm released. "You best not be shittin' on my dick none either. You do, it's you who pulls clean-up duty. You get me?" And just in case you're wondering, I did try to kill him during my time inside, once, but the attempt was by the old me, the Jimmy who Feared. The Jimmy I am now is going to rectify this oversight, having had a good long time to figure things out. I believe that. I really do. And only because there's more than a lovely shade of brown in the bottom of the bowl whenever I stop to wipe.

I also gag if I let myself think about things too much. Hard enough not to, not with how many times I'd been forced to perform. I will change this though, as I think I've said, the outcome I seek worth every goddamn thing they've done to me.

Am I bitter? I counter: Can you fucking blame me?

I have to force these thoughts to the back of my mind though, ensuring they won't fuck up my plans. This is easier said than done and anyone who suggests otherwise is either lying or straight up doesn't know.

"You want me to do what?" said Brady Aldeen. Of my childhood friends he was the last to remain and the second little thing to this plan I have set in motion. And just so we are clear, I didn't like him much, not anymore. The old Jimmy liked him well enough, the one who really couldn't be bothered to put the pieces together and see how he might have ended up in the joint to become Vic's bitch in the first place. This was another thing I was getting better at by approaching life with new eyes; at seeing the forest for the trees. It's liberating really, what it offers a man. I say this not because of what I have learned but because of the opportunity it presents me. All told, they will never see me coming.

"It's only for a night and it's only pretend. Five hundred if you say yes." What I wanted him to do was minor, his role only to get Vic into the car. He had to act the part however, and this was the thing giving Brady second thoughts.

"And you think this guy is gonna believe I'm a queer?" What could I say? That yeah, maybe, especially with the length Brady now kept his hair. Or maybe I go and mention the overly soft features he'd been born with. Maybe that. Instead I lie, saying it would be a hell of a stretch but if anyone could pull it off it'd be him. I also suggest an extra five hundred just to smooth the shit out.

Brady exhaled, closed his eyes. "Make it fifteen and you and me got business."

"You have to be able to sell it though. I mean, this is one mean mother he gets to thinkin' something's up."

"Now you saying I might not be up to snuff?"

"No, I'm just sayin. Christ, Brady. Gimme a bone here. This piece of shit had his way with me for almost a year. If anything, you think you could understand that." For a moment I couldn't believe the words I hear coming from my mouth. Seems I had changed already. Understandable, sure, but be it a good thing or bad was still up for debate.

"Yeah. Yeah. You were his bitch. I get it." I see red as Brady says this, and any second thoughts I might have had in regards to him being the one who ratted me out are out the window and on their way to goddamn fucking Alaska before the man I grew up with removes himself from the bar stool. Hands going hard into his leather jacket I watch as he leaves without looking back.

Who needs enemies, right?

Granted, sucking a man's dick day in and day out for the better part of a year would probably do some damage to even the most resilient of heterosexual minds. This is something I can't quantify completely mind you. But I have to admit such things might be possible. Why else had I so easily lumped Brady into the back part of my plan? Instantaneously choosing to add him to the carnage meant for Vic? Yeah, something had broken inside of me. I just can't give you the words. I can try. And I think I will. I'm just not sure you'll understand. But most of that could be misconstrued, as Brady had always been in the running as the one who sold me out. I might not want to admit this but I have to. The old Jimmy refused this, his fears and the reprisals they could bring allowing the blinders to stay where they were, lapping the shit up. But this is the new me we are talking about, the one who got shit done. So maybe it wasn't so easily I lumped Brady into my plan at all. He was only always meant to die. I just hadn't known it yet.

Or maybe it's just the dreams, the one I wake from colder than I usually am. They are full of penises, these dreams, and they will not stop. Sort of leads me into what I've planned for Vic. If I wanted a chance at any kind of normalcy I was going to have to cut some things out. Trim the fat, so to speak.

Because it concerned Vic, it was going to involve a pretty big knife.

Good for him.

"Back here, man." I could only see the outlines of their bodies because the light in the alley was far from good. Underneath me the ground is wet with rain, it finishing not minutes before I hear Brady and Big Vic's voices coming toward me.

"Your mouth better be ready to take me, boy. That's all you gotta know." I'd heard the speech before, usually before lights out, but this time it would be different. If I wanted any type of life for myself it's what had to happen. Doors shutting, I make my move and slide in the back, right behind Brady. From the passenger's seat up front I see Vic's eyes go wide as he realizes who I am and then that I'm holding a piece.

As the commercials preach: motherfucking priceless.

And I wanted to have a conversation with him; I really did, it too being part of my plan. This was not to be, not as I had hoped. No regaling of what I was about to do or gloating of any kind. Just screaming as the rage inside me steps forward and proves it has a mind of its own. Just pop-pop into each of them and then each of them goes forward. I have to pull Brady back to stop the horn from blaring but in the end it's no real biggie. Vic's penis is the exact opposite of this and I smile as I tighten the lid to the jar it still now rests in. Brady's too is now behind glass but the size of his jar is better suited to jams. Each now sit on my bedside table, there for me to admire. I should be getting rid of them, both pieces being evidence and all, but I'm finding it hard to part with what I've done. This upsets me more than I think it should. Worrying me for reasons contrary to what I've already said; that by changing the way I approached things I might be able to purge certain tendencies inherent to my life. This has yet to happen. Not as I hoped it would. One step beyond is what scares me even more.

What if I just like sucking dick now? Fuck, what if I always have?

GANK

It started when they found the fourth girl, her throat another mouth. Only it didn't. It started two years earlier with a girl named Rebecca Hall.

Blue eyes. Honey Hair. But for everything she was, Batista said her dog was what neighbors remembered most; that the talkative little white girl who lived in the crack house on Brock was always on about it never getting enough to eat even though the same could be said of her. Habit, they said. The good kind.

Sad, she was eaten herself. By a monster Culver P.D. had yet to radar. The day they do it's Rebecca's crack-pipe parents making the most noise of all.

"You'd think this have happened sooner," Batista spits to the ground as he says this, impatient as I've ever seen him. "Pieces of shit probably looking to cash."

I couldn't disagree. Seen it too many times to believe otherwise.

Victim number five is what provides the link. Marilyn Sims. Tall and sweet. Proud and loud. All but sixteen. Inside her stomach was what remained of the family dog, a collie named Frank. From there it's only a matter of time.

Batista and the rest of the department get to work. Dog walkers. Groomers. Vet and pre-vet. Anyone who'd enrolled and then dropped the field within the last five years. Eventually the investigation focuses on kennels, their owners, and then especially it's a man name of Gank who's looked at hard.

Sunny smile. Sweet disposition. Co-operative until he wasn't.

A record as long as my days are bleak.

B&E. Possession. Possession with intent. Rapes first, second, and third degree.

Inheriting the business from an uncle, the piece of scum comes to Culver three years prior by way of over-crowding, early release and a probation system down for the count. Business still in his uncle's name, it's the perfect front. My take, anyway.

A new home, he must have thought. New things.

Things he'd yet to try.

"You got maybe an hour before the warrant is good and we go in." I told Batista I'd worked with less; that I would again. A different storm was approaching, though. One I had seen coming from a long ways away.

"You're wrong in thinking I enjoy this. I'm not like you." It was a bone between Batista and me, old and gnawed on by years.

"Isn't about enjoyment, John; it's about what's right." Opposite sides of the coin we may be, I could not be-grudge the man—the detective yet to have someone of importance to him ripped from his life like a bone from your arm. These choices—these are the ones which allow me to sleep at night.

"Ensure he suffers. That's all I'll say."

He didn't have to.

Once I connect the positives I let the engine run for minutes at a time. Gank, no longer sweet, no longer sunny, and infinitely less co-operative than I'd been told, shits himself by time the second go-round. After that he spills like a baby, his balls a smoking mess. He also goes religious on me, which is not so out of the norm. Once they realize what I represent...once they know, it's usually all *our fathers full of grace* and *repent, repent, repent.* Horseshit, you ask me. You kill, you die. Simple as that.

"I'm sick," he says, blood now leaking from his eyes. He's on his back, hands bound, pants around his shins. "My head, it doesn't work right."

I let him know I'll be fixing that.

Latisha Kennedy and Jenny McGovern would find their way home. That's the only reason I hadn't put two in the back of his head the moment I found him packing his things. I could have. Easily. The rage I felt toward the man no longer hot but arctic; couldn't un-think what he'd done and how he'd left them.

What stopped me was the need to know.

And if it'd been my child.

One way or another I would bring them closure. That

was how I rationalized it. What the parents of the unfound girls deserved at the very least.

Not even close to fair by far, but then again, this is Culver, a place God had yet to apply.

THE ONLY THING THAT FITS

Four boys playing fort found what we'd thought was the second girl, Rebecca Hall, age twelve, beat, bloodied, and dead. Last time anyone had seen her was two days prior, a Monday, two steps off her school bus and sixty from home. Deputy Detective John Batista is the officer who catches the case, me, in turn, becoming his very next call. A murderer in my own right, I had no problem doing what needed to be done. Batista, giant, thick, with a face the color of pissed-off brick, knew this as well. Both of us more than proficient in the art of subterfuge we'd come to utilize. Seeing we were the very same thing we'd come to hunt meant we pretty much had to be.

The autopsy confirmed what each of us feared: rape. What it also confirmed was that Rebecca Hall was not the second victim but actually the fourth. Not to be done, it was the girl's stomach content which s₁ loudest of all.

"It's canine, Rider. Goddamn bastard fed her her dog." Even strong men had bad days. For Batista, this was one. "A collie named Frank."

"Narrows it down though, way I see it." I was right, of course, and Batista knew as much. Didn't mean either of us he had to like it. Scenarios just worked better this way. Same thing with plans.

Three weeks later—after every vet, pre-vet, canine shelter, dog walker, and pet food store owner are interviewed from Culver City down to Hanson Falls—it's a man by the name of Gank the CCPD looks at hard. Inheriting his kennel by way of an uncle who held a different last name, Rudy Gank had come to Culver three years prior by way of overcrowding, early release and a probation system down for the count. Wasn't much of a surprise either, the circumstance one the core reasons the detective and I had begun what we had.

Text message received, I find the piece of scum in jeans and a beater T. Thick and wide, he's packing a bag in an attempt to flee. It's as he turns around that I tell him to lie on the ground.

"You ain't no cop." Man had me there.

"By the time I'm done with you, Rudy, I can guarantee you'll wish I was."

Fuck and *you* were the next things that tried to come from his mouth. Once he regained consciousness I'd already connected jumper cables that stretched from balls to battery and back again. Juice turned up, the man fries, the world becoming a slightly better place in the process.

Or so I'd thought.

"It's happening again," Batista says, and the look in the man's eyes tells me more than I care to know. Turns out Gank had a sibling, a brother, Henry J. Seems Henry J liked the same things Rudy did, right down to feeding his victims a lighter shade of pink.

"I mean, you can't be fucking serious." It was rhetorical, and Batista had said it more than a few times since we'd uncovered the link. We were at the usual spot, each of us looking down over Culver as it slept.

"Doesn't make a difference, John. Once we find him, man's going to die all the same."

"I know. I know. But Gank having a partner, a brother no less, and us missing that, it makes me think I might be getting too old for this." I've seen a lot of things, more than I care to acknowledge. One thing I know for certain is that true evil is more human than mankind will ever come to admit. It also lives only to destroy. Batista knew as much, was the reason he wore the badge, but it also proved that he and I were as different now as we'd been back then.

"John. The man will slip up. We'll get him. I promise."

And we did, just not as I thought we would, nor when. Four years and eleven girls later I get the call. Batista. He's at a safe house of mine, one of the bigger ones, telling me he'd finally struck gold. I move, and fast, as there was something in the big man's voice. Shouldn't have surprised me though, what I found, as the case had taken its toll on Batista, whittling him down bit by bit these last couple years. Empathy and ineffectiveness will do that to a cop. Sadly, each is capable of creating the worst type of fuse.

"Stop...no...too deep!" is what comes to me once I

open up the floor. The screams accompanying the words are high and full, erupting from a mouth that can hardly catch what it needs to breathe. What hits me next is the smell of shit that is wet and fresh and round. As for Batista, he's there within it, Henry Gank's pants about his shins, his face against the wall, and Batista up inside him with a piece of rebar that could have passed for bone.

Batista is grunting, a man determined, but he is weeping as well, and it is here I lay a hand upon his back, and then upon his wrist, and then he all at once stops and relinquishes the steel.

"I tried, Rider...thought I could..." he says, and I know how he needs it to end. I've always known. But we weren't the same, never have been and never would be. I'd like to say I envy him that, but no, I've too much hate.

"I'll finish," I say and then send Batista up a level to clean up as much of himself as he could. Once I hear the floor door close is when I step toward a face so close to one I thought I'd never see again. He'd made his way to a corner, a trail of shit and blood snaking the concrete between us. I hunker down, face him, and tell him of his brother; of how that piece of scum had burned and wept and pled before I ripped apart his eyes.

The man starts, snarls, but then stops just as quick, and I can only assume it's because Batista had taken too much from him. Never one to look a gift horse in the mouth, I too take something from the man, his jaw, by way of hammer, but before I do he tries his best to stand. Once up, he glares at me, finally choosing to speak. "Like I tole your friend, why we did it, why we do, it's because even dirty bitches need to eat." It's only when the silence comes that I realize the time for talking had already passed.

For those of us who know, it's the only thing that fits.

LOOSE IMPEDIMENT

I have two loves in this life: the game and my wife. I am bad at one and not so good at the other. Until recently, I did not know this. Not until my P.I. gave me the footage.

Truth be told, I never would have envisioned Sharon doing something like this, not sensible-shoe Sharon, the woman of my dreams. Others, yes, but not the saucer-eyed red-head I met my sophomore year. Looking back though, it gives you what they say: hindsight. Fuck, does it. I mean, the irony of this thing, it's just a beast, like full fucking throttle and then some.

I'll calm down now.

"We never *do* anything together," Sharon states, one of her favorites. Another such gem: "Is this all there is?" I realize the second statement says more about Sharon's state of mind than I'd like, but this is what you do when it comes to people you love. You make concessions. Now that I think about it, this might say more about *me* than I'd like. Does it matter though? Now, after everything that's been done? I don't think so, not in the greater scheme of things. Saying shit like that, this is the shit that gets you punched, isn't it?

Thought so.

So Dave is the guy. Head pro at the country club I'm a member of. He wasn't smarmy per se, but he did project that car salesman vibe: perfect teeth and such, always smiling in a way which seemed overly wide. As for handshakes, he was absolutely that guy: over hard and attempting to crush. The piece of shit rarely called me by my name either, always giving me a Skip or Ace instead of what he should. It bugged me, sure, but did I speak up? Hell no, not once I've given myself the opportunity to downplay events. This is nothing new, of course, as confrontation and I have never gotten along, not as we should. I made up this last part, and only because I'm more of a revisionist than what one would call a classic avoider. Take your pick though, because either is good for the reason I find myself where I do. I will not take the brunt though, not the majority, and only because it wasn't me who'd been found with another man's dick down their throat.

Am I done? No. But I'll go on.

Me, I've always been bad at golf, awful, but I love it anyway. Can't get enough really. Sharon, unfortunately, was worse than me when it came to the sport. Long story short, I was informed that she and Dave would need a little more one-on-one time if she were to ever get better. Stupid, I know. But we never "did" things together, right? And to tell you the truth, I think I already knew. Deep inside is what I'm saying, like the shit that comes up in your dreams.

Speaking of dreams—in one I see Dave as I always see

him, there on the range, his perfect teeth so perfectly fucking perfect, but this time he's right tight behind the woman I call wife, Sharon's hair for some reason shorter and darker than she usually keeps it. I notice her foot wear as well—that it's as far from sensible as the word can stretch. (This scared me more than anything, and I'm pretty sure I know why. What it represents, anyway. I'm not saying I'm any type of Freud either, it's just when the writing on the wall is that big and that glowing even I had to take my head from the sand.) Dave's arms come around her then; Sharon's making their way around the club. Moaning, they find a rhythm I seldom have, each practice swing like an orgasm unto no other.

Wait. It gets better.

Two other things I see before I wake up. My wife's face full of a pleasure I have never seen, not once. The other is the bulge in Dave's khakis. I am not exaggerating when I say this. Baby. Fucking. Elephant. Don't get me wrong, I'm no jackhammer, but put me up beside what I was witnessing and man, even I felt gherkin. Gherkin-esqe?

Do I say anything in this dream? Stand up for what I thought of as mine? Just as in real life, no. As this is what it means to be me. Therein lies the problem, I think, and quite possibly the root of my evil. Maybe. Maybe not. Either way, it boils down to this: Did I deserve it?

I was about to find out.

It's why I now had Dave in my garage, the man's cargo shorts a little worse for wear. Secured to a circular practice net like an X, he looked at me differently now, with slightly wider than normal eyes. Many a night have I been out here plugging away, all to no avail. Not in all my years, with all my practice, have I gotten better at this game I love. Sucks hard, this, but I am at least man enough to admit as much.

"We going to be able to have a civilized conversation once I remove the tape, Dave?" Dave nods yes, sweat-beads up upon his brow.

"Chris, dude, what the fuck?"

"Don't Dave…just…don't." It's here that I strike the right tone, as the man, still suspended, slumps forward, dejected.

"It's not like we were planning to," is what he says next, although his voice is quiet now, reserved even. I didn't care, not really, just wanted a little bit of fear from the man, that's all. Pretty sure I was owed a little something along those lines. Maybe a smidge more.

"So you know how you've been trying to teach me that draw, Dave?" A draw is a right-to-left ball flight for a right-handed golfer. It is very hard to produce and highly sought after. According to Dave, it's what breaks or makes careers.

I didn't let him answer. I re-applied the tape instead. Then I set up a ball on the practice mat ten feet in front of the man who'd been fucking my wife. It is here I picture his dick from my dreams, the one bigger than God, and it's here I envision it entering Sharon, filling her up from behind as only a man with a bigger dick than me could do. It is enough. More than enough. It is the end.

"Thing is, I finally got it," I say, referring to what he'd been trying to teach me. "It's funny though, you know—that it took what you and Sharon have done to 'draw' it out of me." A comedian I was not, but I laughed anyway. Then I took a practice swing. All loosened up, I took two more. Done with those and it was on to the main event: one hundred and sixteen golf balls dead on until the man's teeth were no longer perfect. His orbital bones took a beating as well, each one ending up with their very own logo. Pretty sweet seeing that. For sure.

As for Sharon? She of the sensible shoes? With her it would have to be something different. Something large and in charge.

A slice, perhaps.

.

KNOWN ASSOCIATES

Hang on; lemme swing this chair around.

Okay. There. Now as I said, I have a story to tell. It's not my story, it's not your story, but we've become a part of it regardless. Call it chance or fate or whatever the fuck you want, but be sure, we are ingredients and nothing more. You ready then? Good. Time to fuckin' do this!

The first time I meet Bishop Rider he puts the back of Marty Abrum's head through the front of his nose in the restaurant I'm working at. I'm a busboy slash dish-washer at this restaurant and had been bussing tables the night this shit goes down. Before Abrum's head becomes part of his pasta Rider takes out the other three guys surrounding Marty in a blink-and-you'll-miss-it kind of scenario. I mean, just pop, pop, pop, and then a whole buncha screams from all the other guests as they go and say their whatnots to the floor. Next comes the shotgun, pulled from an overcoat as dark as the big man's hair. Sawed off, Rider places it downwards on the back of Marty's thin head. I hear *for my sister* and then BOOM, bone and marinara sauce become two great tastes that taste great together.

You old enough to remember that one, Richie?

Anyway…do I do anything? Sure I do. Pretty sure I stand as still as I possibly can as my mouth does its best impression of a cave. I mean, the heat offa this guy, the anger, it came in shimmers I thought I could fucking see. And you've heard the stories, I know you have, about how the Abrum brothers abducted or had someone abduct Rider's sister and mother and then had the mother killed while the sister is fucked to death by a buncha oversized dudes in masks. Fucked to death? I know. Can you imagine? It's what the brothers were into though, and making what I'm told they called their "special films." How April and Maggie Rider become involved with what usually only consisted of smuggled Mexican women I guess we'll never know.

Or perhaps we will. I mean, it is just us here, right?

Brings me to the second time I meet Bishop Rider. The dude comes out from the shadows as I'm putting my key to the lock of my place. Almost gives me a goddamn heart attack is what this does. He's as big as I remember him and twice as fucking angry. And yes, yes, to look at he reminds you of Frank Castle, minus a skull on his chest of course, but whereas that bulldozer of a fuck is a work of fiction this former cop is as real as the meat shovel he has up around my neck. Against the wall, he begins to ask me things, Richie, people things, and then known associates goes and enters the conversation.

Now why, pray tell, would something like this happen, Richie?

Could it involve something you might want to get off your chest?

'S'okay. I think we'll leave the gag right where it is. Truth be told, I got this. You see, once I realized what the man was about, well, you know me and you, we ain't ever been the tightest of compadres, but we've been alright with one another. Small jobs here and there but never with nobody ever getting hurt. This is me, always has been me. I might be soft for it, sure, but it has always allowed me to sleep at night. You, though? You went and upgraded yourself to the big leagues, didn't you?

What I mean to say is this: Was there anyone else with you in the van that day? A simple nod will do. Richie? Honor among thieves, really? You know that's just a buncha made up bullshit the movies would have you believe.

He found surveillance, Richie.

He knows *your* brother was with you when it went down.

I've also seen the footage and I see the predicament you found yourself in. I'm guessing the Mexican girls in the back of the van somehow jimmy the lock from the inside. Good for them. Seriously. But I also see that Bishop's sister has parked too close to the back of your van, the arms of the women trying to escape the only appendages coming to see the light of day. You shoulda took off is what I think you should have done, but no, you herd the sister and the mother into the van at gun-point and now here we are, you on your couch and me in your face. Effectively, you and your brother put this entire thing in motion. You see that? Sure, the reins were taken over by the Abrum boys once the situation was brought to their attention, but you guys, you are the ones responsible for what it unleashed.

Brings us to now, the fourth time I meet Bishop Rider. Didn't even hear them big black boots come up behind you, did you, Richie? And yes, that object you feel is exactly what you think it is; the very same shotgun I told you about earlier. Seems to be pointing a little lower than it did on Marty Abrum, I think, perhaps into the small of your neck it looks like. You know what that means? Means your face and acrobats are about to have more than a whole lot in common. Before we paint the coffee table though…before we do I think it might be fair for you to hear about the third time Bishop Rider enters my life. I mean, in the bigger scheme of things, I *can* see it being pertinent to what's about to unfold. It's not much, not really, but sometimes not much is all you ever truly need.

I meet Batista, Rider's contact on the inside, and it's here that three like-minded individuals decide to take it upon themselves to do what most in this world will not.

Last thing, Richie: once you've caught up to him, tell your brother we made good on our word. His dogs, they ate like kings.

COFFEE, TEA AND ME

Looking back, I never would have guessed I could be this type of person. In my opinion, it proves the existence of God, or at least narrows the implication of him; that we do have free will. It is only because of this rationale that I carry on.

I believe there are two types of people in this world: those who drink coffee and those who drink tea. How they drink their choice, well, that's where most of the problems lie. From early on I've been a tea drinker, same as my wife. Often I would ready Cara a hot cup for when she exited the shower. She never asked me to do this—it was just something I would do.

Cara and I met in college, she in her final year of admin, me just about to complete my bachelor's in popular science. As they say, the sparks flew—and oh how we danced. Times change though—don't get me wrong, I'm not saying I am adverse to such things. Quite the opposite, matter of fact, as I know it is a part of life. What I am trying to convey is that we were no more special than anyone else, and that after twelve years of marriage there are bound to be some bumps in the road.

Bumps. yes Mountains, no.

47

"What's wrong with Mommy?" That is Leighton. She is eight now and came four years after Cara and I became husband and wife. Except for her chin, she is a mirror to her mother, right down to the curl of her dark brown hair.

"Mommy's sick," I say. Which was true, and enough to keep Cara from work and in bed for the better part of the month. We sat at the kitchen table, my daughter and I, bowls of frosted flakes in front of us both.

"I know she's sick," Leighton says. "It's just…"

"Different?" I suggest, and suddenly recognize my daughter's strength for what it is; that she is much smarter than I had previously thought. Deep down she knows something is off. Some part of her anyway. Keeping cool I change the subject, ask on about *iCarly* and the Montana girl. It works, our discussion soon turning toward school and the getting ready for it. At the bus, before she gets on, Leighton asks, "She won't die, Daddy, will she?"

Did I lie?

Did I tell the truth?

I did neither, realizing I was now more than ever the man I never thought I would become. Granted, I had been well on my way, but by not answering Leighton's question, well, that just solidified it all together. *Gelled* it, actually.

"You needn't worry about such things," I said, and then waved her on her way. Turning, I stopped, took in the view of our house, thought about what lay inside. She was dying, yes, and it was clearly because of me, but it was also because of her—that is what I want known most of all. Not because Cara lived the life of a naturopath, but because of what she did. She will never admit as such, not outright, and for truth I would never ask her to; this just us being us.

Things began to turn around the time Cara began mentioning a new co-worker at the office, this new guy named Mike; my take on it anyway. After a retreat her entire floor went on was when it hit home, however; when this Mike was no longer mentioned in the stories of Cara's day. What clinched it were the blowjobs I began waking up to not long after. I chalk this up to guilt, as this was Cara's way. Not that I minded, there at the start, but when I really sat down to contemplate the reason for the extra attention I was receiving some mornings...

This is when I think I began to turn, the moment and place.

Was my tea not good enough anymore? Yes, this thought did go through my mind. So did, was it coffee she wanted now? Is that the way it was? I didn't know, couldn't know, and seemed to be standing beside myself, our lives together running through my mind at a gallop. I see her smiling, laughing, dancing; see her cooing, sighing, frowning. I see it all, our entire life, the good as well as the bad. This is life, I think, what everything's all about. And then I see her drinking tea, the tea I make and leave on the counter for her to have after her shower. I do this because I love her, so she would never have to wait. I picture her dumping it then, there in the toilet, there in my mind, and this is where the coffee comes forth, my analogy of the damned. It is more than I can take, hence what I have done.

Cara turns toward the light as I open the door. The room is dark and has begun to smell.

"How are you feeling?" Better, she says, but her voice betrays her calm. It is because of this stubbornness that I will get away with what I have done. Her family has been here, mine as well, but Cara, God love her, will not budge, not even here, when we find ourselves at the end. It was the same thing with Leighton's birth; that no modern medicine would touch our child's head.

"No. No," I say. "Don't try to get up." She ignores me, stumbles, but I am far enough into the room that I catch her in time. Sitting up, I pass her the tea that I have brought. She smiles, says thanks, and sends a hand to stroke my stubbled cheek. For a moment I pause and think I hear the man I used to be; that he is protesting from somewhere very far away. The moment passes, as moments do, and then it is only Cara and I, sitting as we have come to do.

"It's bitter," Cara states, her smile weak, her body weaker.

I agree, telling her the flavor is new. What I don't tell her is I no longer have the wherewithal to mask the taste.

"Oolong-almond? Who'd have thought?"

"Yes," I say. "Who indeed."

RECOMPENSE

You may remember Gabe Weller, you may not. In his twenties he does what was done to my parents and takes a red-handled axe to both his mother and father as they sleep. Post-apprehension, he comes to say, yes, okay, it was in fact his body that did the deed, but his mind was a whole other story. All this comes to light after video surveillance of a car matching his is found leaving through the front of his parents' gated community. This in addition to footage and a receipt of him purchasing shoes two sizes too small two nights before the murders occur. If one were to hazard a guess, it doesn't take much to realize the size of footprints discovered in the blood that is collected and catalogued. That was then, however, and what I wish to address is now.

How Gabe Weller seems to have found God.

We are sixteen years removed from said incident, sure, and I can only assume the amount of time it took for Gabe to embrace and concoct all he would need for when he's finally released. It happens though, all of it, and the notoriety the man creates for himself, well, this is what led him to me.

Dressed for weather, toque pulled tight, he fails to

hear me come up from behind as he makes his way to his car following a book signing. As it should, the hypodermic does everything it needs to. Out of the van I introduce the left side of his face to a doorway in an attempt to remove the man's goatee. When it doesn't work I give it another four tries. Six more and I almost have what I'm looking for.

Upon waking, I tell him the tape is there for a reason—that it's because he's lost the goddamn right. Done, I pull him higher, tighter, ensuring he's as taut as he can be. I use chains now, opposed to rope, as the sound that accompanies the sway seems to elicit in them a fear far greater than expected.

"You say you believe in intelligent design. That God exists." He does not even nod, only looks at me with eyes as wide as doorknobs. They are beaten, bruised and bloodshot, but even then they match what only certain men will see: they have been caught by something outside their pre-conceived notions.

"And the arrogance you possess, to believe that all of this, everything, that it has been made specifically for you. It's beyond arrogant, really." Did he know what I was on about? Did I care? Not really. What concerned me more was how he'd turned what he did to his favor; that religion found him a way. It's as insane as telling a six-year-old he or she will burn eternally if they choose to not believe.

Yes, my hate doth grow.

It's why I produce a red-handled axe and begin to ask Gabe Weller different kinds of questions. Ones he was sure to steer clear of in that book of his. Wasn't until I got to the end of things that he realized what I'd been up to.

Eye for an eye, I say. Followed by time heals no wounds, served or otherwise. I don't start up top though, choosing instead to stack the man like wood. Arms on top the pile I say out loud his parent's names.

It would have to do.

BOBBY CHARLES

"Was it worth it?" There in the gloom, this is what he asked. It was also not the first time he'd asked the question since waking me. Fumbling for a response, the flood gates opened, and this was when I came to know exactly with whom I was dealing; that there would be no coming back, not the same way I came, anyway. And in situations like those, I knew they tended to hurry.

I couldn't blame him though, not really, and once you hear how everything went down you will understand why. Why he did what he did, and why I choose to live with it. I mean, the dude had every right in the book to end me, and if the shoe had been on the other foot, well, I can't say for sure that I would've been able to show the same amount of restraint that Bobby did. No, not for sure. I'm not saying I'm a coward; no, but I will convey that I've never truly been tested. There is a difference. Of this at least I know.

He was angry. Livid actually, and it seemed to permeate off of him in waves. It was not quite dawn, but the night was leaving just the same. He sat in the chair opposite my bed, the one I used for day-old clothes. His legs were crossed and his arms ran the length of each arm of said chair. I could see he took care of himself and that he went to a gym. In the past I have done this myself, enjoying the release I found in lifting the weights. Lately, though? Not so much. Now there is an extra layer to my mid-section. It matches the one above my neck.

His eyes are what captured me. Sunken and blue, they were rimmed by dark circles. There was a redness there, too, a rawness. I assume this comes from the kind of crying one finds themselves unable to stop. I do not think I am very far off in this assessment. The man looked broken is what I mean to say, but he appeared coiled as well—like I said, I could *feel* his anger. Looking back, I now realize he was only ever these two things with me—sorrow and rage—and I could complain about that until I was blue in the face, but I don't think I will, as I deserve everything this man has done to me. However, I will say this: I am sure he is not the first person to eat of those two emotions. I am also sure he will not be the last.

"I said, *was it worth it?*" The man was all business, straight and to the point from beneath the visor of his ball cap. I looked at him, silent, unable to do anything but go over everything I had read about him during my stay in the hospital: Bobby Charles, father of one, husband of almost ten years. Age: forty-five, nineteen years my senior. He enjoyed fishing and golf and owned a restaurant which he ran up on Brock. The Pita Pit is what I think it's called. He was a widower now, of course, and the only reason for that was because of me, yours truly. I'd cost him his son as well. The boy…his name had been Patrick.

I did not kill these people on purpose, no, but do not doubt that it is my fault just the same.

I tried to answer him but found myself unable. Pausing, I remember thinking, What did he want from me, anyway? Would his lawyers not be taking me for everything I owned soon enough? Was the cost of me breaking both my legs in the accident not payment enough? Even as I thought it, I regretted it—whole-hearted and immediate. If anything, I have learned a lot about myself because of that day. Chief amongst them being this: I was more selfish than I could have ever imagined. And denial is very much a form of addiction. Not the *big* denial, the type which can get you through serious trauma, but the everyday denials we incorporate into life. The ones which let us believe we are good people, if only we *choose* to believe.

I cleared my throat, swallowed, and then adjusted the pillow between my back and the headboard as best I could. As they'd been doing for a while, my legs protested this. Bobby and me? We continued to look at each other, to blink and breathe. We listened as well, as the clock above the door frame went tick, tick, tick. Finally, I asked: "Will you kill me?"

He only shook his head and repeated, "Was it worth it?" And then I realized that his head nod was not an answer to whether or not he was here to kill me. He wanted his question answered is all; didn't want the jerk in front of him answering it with one of his own. Why would he? This wasn't about me—well, okay, it was; how could it not be?—but this is not the point I am trying to make. What I am attempting to show is how narcissistic I was, how self-absorbed and shallow. This is what I want you to know, that it wasn't until he did what he did that I truly understood what it all was ever supposed to be about. Funny, isn't it? What it takes to open one's eyes? No, not funny—sad; pathetic, really.

Still, the question remained. *Was it worth it?* Was *what* worth it? That is what I wanted to say, as I had no idea to what his question referred. I was at least smart enough—and scared enough—to realize that I had to get on with it and finally just ask him what the fuck he meant. The whole thing here, he in the chair, me waking up to him in the chair, it had taken no more than six minutes, seven on the outside. I can tell you it did not *feel* like minutes. No, it felt more like hours.

"Mr. Charles," I said. "I am not trying to upset you, but, man, I don't really understand what it is you're asking me. Clearly I am in no position to assume…" And we were back to regarding each other, he and his eyes simmering, me in my bed wondering if he was asking me if it was killing his son and wife that was worth it? Was this the question he was asking?

He said, "I was behind you, Randy—on the road when it happened. Did you know that?"

And all of a sudden I knew; could not *not* know; envisioned myself driving that day, driving as I always drove, like I was the only one who mattered.

It happened on Main, a four-lane black-top which is

one of the busiest in the city. It's also a street where between the hours of eight a.m. and four p.m., between the first and fifteenth of any given month, cars are allowed to park. The day it all went down? March eighth; a Tuesday. And you can rest assured that it happened well within the aforementioned eight-hour window.

"No," I said, finally answering his question. I was really answering both his questions, but I'm still not sure if he was aware of this or not. Either way, my response had been something just short of a whisper. For the first time since he arrived I found myself unable to hold his gaze as well. Guilt has a way of doing this, I'm finding.

"If you had made it, you would've just carried on. I know this. This is what people like you do. It's how you're wired. Out for no one but yourself." The anger remained, but he had control of it, seemed to be almost chewing on the words as he said them to me. In hindsight, he was doing the best that he could. I see that now. Actually, I see a lot of things now. One such gem is this: if I hadn't killed his wife and child, I would have scoffed at the accusation he presented, if not outright denied it. *That* was how far gone I was in believing myself a good person. And if that is not as fucked as it gets, I do not know what is.

But I did kill his wife and I did kill his child.

I wasn't going to wait; my time more precious than anyone's; that is what it came down to.

I had been passing and speeding. I had been dodging and weaving. Many of us do this, unable to obey the posted limit; always *on* our way. The morning that it happened, nothing was different. If anything I was probably a little slow to speed up as I went to change lanes that final time. This is what it hinged on, that I tried to cut over when I should have slowed. But if I had slowed, I would then have to wait for an opening and signal my way through. This would not do. I would not wait. After all, it was *my* world we were living in.

I cut over, clipped her minivan, sending them and the van headlong into the teeth of an eighteen-wheeler. The big machine ate. The grill, I'm told, coming to hold bone. Myself? I over-corrected the clip and hit a patch of black ice. As you can imagine, coming out of the slide at the speed I was going—let's just say that the flips I did were far from few.

"You're a liar as well as a murderer. You know that?"

I re-found his gaze, looked up and slowly nodded my response. I was caught, and had been since he got there—denial or no denials.

"First sensible thing you've done since I got here."

"If you saw me…" I said, now curious. "Why haven't you told the police?"

"Does it matter?" He spat his answer, and then leaned forward in the chair. "Whatever. You want to know, I'll tell you. I was waiting for you. Not at first. At first I was in shock. But as the investigation went on I came to realize what you were up to. Or rather, what you were omitting in your statement. This is when I knew you for a liar. You are a coward, too, Randy."

Suddenly his anger abated. There in the chair, his shoulders sank and he began to cry. His eyes looked weary now, and his voice—it lost the grate it bore, the fury. "I never once heard you mention how you were darting in and out of traffic that day. Not once that your speed...that it was well above what it was supposed to be. Sure you said you were going a little over the posted, but nothing like what I saw. You *know* what I saw? I saw a man who couldn't care less about those around him; a man who at best is a child. You were an accident waiting to happen. And you know what the funny thing is, out of all of this. I thought that very thing as I watched you pass me that morning, not thirty seconds before..."

His voice had become quiet and, as I said, anger-free. He was a different Bobby Charles than the one I had been dealing with. This was the shell of that man, his husk. I was sure the other one still lurked there somewhere, but for the time being he was nowhere to be seen.

"No," I said again. "No, Mr. Charles, it wasn't worth it. I know that now. Actually, it should have been something I knew before what happened happened; which would have prevented it from happening, now that I think about it. But in regards to the statement I gave to the police..."

"Don't! Don't go there." And like that, his fury was back. Restrained but oh so on fire. "You said what you said. That it wasn't worth it. Good, it's what I needed to hear. It makes what comes next much easier. In the meantime, don't go digging yourself holes you can't climb out of."

"Bobby, please, let me at least explain why—"

"Do *not* call me Bobby!"

"Sorry. I'm sorry. I just…" but my words, they failed me. And I believe it was right about then that everything started to clear for me; this moment when I began to look at life from a whole new angle. I believe this is called a paradigm shift. Is this correct? Whatever you called it—this was when my "rampant" apathy and "masked" sociopathic tendencies found themselves beneath the boot heel of the human condition, quashed forevermore.

It was the beginning of my change for the better.

"It doesn't matter," he said, his anger dissipating once more. He sighed. "We are where we are; are what we are. The road less travelled. Whatever." And then he laughed, but there was no humor in it. No; none. "Sometimes I think it was as much my fault as it is yours. I used to have a mantra….a saying I'd whisper to myself whenever I would get thinking about things, when things like losing my wife and child to inexplicable random events crept into my head. It started when Val and I were dating, from there snowballing to include our son. They never knew I did this, even when the need arose and I found myself in the same room with either of them. I would turn my head, quietly repeat my phrase three times, and that would be it. But I had to mean it, that was the thing, the promise I set for myself. I could never just go through the motions. If I did, it wouldn't work, and whatever I had tricked myself into believing would fail, ensuring the inexplicable random events which scared the shit out of me could do nothing more than come true; stupid; all of it. But it kept me going, believing. And then you came. Randy McAlister—my Mr. Inexplicable."

I didn't know what to say, didn't know what to do. *Should I comment?* ran through my head. So did begging for my life. Instead I watched him stand up and take off his ball cap. He looked to the window, ran a hand through what remained of his hair. At this I realized how empty the man was; how much I had emptied him. Turning from the window, he said, "Earlier you asked me if I'd kill you. Honestly, that's what I came here to do. In my head I was going to give you one chance, one question: was it worth it. You answered the question, Randy, but you didn't answer it correctly. To tell you the truth, I don't believe you fully comprehend the query. But as we sat here, as we talked, something occurred to me. I'm here for a reason—to give you *more* time, not take it. You need to know. You need to see."

He left the room then, his big work boots heavy on the floor. He wasn't gone a long time, it only felt that way—the minutes like hours. I don't know for sure, but he might have even done this on purpose—making me wait like he did. Maybe so, maybe no. Either way, the man was certainly entitled. Anyway, it was only a feeling.

The screen door slammed shut as he came back in. It had been old, that door, and loud, in need of repair since before I inherited the place from my parents. It was as the axe hit the floor with a thud that my balls hardened and my penis shrank. At this time I didn't know it was the axe from the woodpile outback he had brought back inside with him, remember, only that an object of considerable weight had been grounded to my kitchen floor. He dragged it too, the whole way back. Picture him doing this: the handle, his hand. Now picture red paint, but faded from years of use. The noise it made? It became the stuff of nightmares to me, of *can't believe* and *this is not happening!* It put mice in my chest and ice down my back. And again it seemed as though he were taking his time, making sure I had everything I needed to completely take in the sound which approached me. He probably *was* doing this, but I'll never know, not for sure. The old me? The person I used to be? He would say this was *exactly* what Bobby Charles was doing, the old dog getting himself a bit of an hors d'oeuvre before the main course to come; his big 'ole slice of retribution pie. Oh yes, my old self could see this very well.

Curious: I didn't scream. And, looking back, I cannot for the life of me find a reason why this wouldn't happen. Is it possible to become too scared to scream? I don't know, but I would probably prove a very good case study.

So I didn't scream. Instead, I watched the doorway until he came back into view. As he did, I saw the axe, it trailing behind him like a long and rigid pet. It wasn't until seeing this image that I realized why the terror inside me had been building. It was the sound, you see, the dragging, scraping sound which accompanied the man's return. I think deep down I might have known what it was all along. Right here, at this realization, was when my bladder let go.

"Don't worry," he said and came toward me, forward, to the edge of my bed. The axe was up in one hand now, held onto by the neck. He pointed it at me as he talked; little jabbing motions which seemed to punctuate every third word or so. "This is not what I had in mind. No, I brought a gun. One I was going to put in your mouth and make you eat. This will not be happening now."

His anger? The stuff he had brought with him? Gone. Not an ounce of it in him now. It wasn't lurking either, as before, when his display of emotions were back and forth, both fast and furious. No, something had happened. He was calm now. Dejected, but calm. Soon I would come to know why; to find that the man had found an escape route—me, of course, the in-house facilitator.

We looked at the axe, both from different perspectives. His most likely reverence, mine most definitely fear. He hefted the weight in front of me, changed hands then grabbed it by the neck once more. Back to punctuating, he said, "I won't lie. This won't be easy on you. Going to hurt like nothing you have ever felt, I'm sure. However, when it's over, I will leave you a choice. Might not seem fair to you, but you are a murderer, Randy. I don't want you to ever forget that. This is why it has to be this way; this your daily reminder. Ready?"

Ready for what? This is what I wanted to say; what I needed to say. A mewling sound came out of me instead, the back of my skull suddenly trying its very best to push through the headboard it was up against.

As he raised the axe I raised my arms.

Down it came, down, and fire erupted in my mind as big black spots popped into my field of vision. This time I *did* scream, but it sounded far away and high—like a girl's. He took off his belt next, creating a tourniquet half way down my thigh. Vaguely I remember him asking where I kept my own, or if I even used one. I couldn't answer, or if I did, I have blocked it out. He must have found one though, as I didn't bleed out once he went around the bed to finish what he started. What I do remember him saying is this: "You took two from me, now I have taken the same from you." Then I felt metal in my hand, the gun he placed there. Down in my ear now, he spoke as I writhed in pain and screamed in curses. "I will give you one chance. I will stand and swing one last time. I will aim for your head. Do me this one thing right, Randy. Send me home. I miss them. More than I could have ever known. If I do it myself, I chance them again. That is something I cannot do—"

I shot him right about there, before he stood up, before his final swing. And I emptied the gun, but you already know this part of the story. Do you want to know how his body jerked backward as well? That his arms flew out but his ball cap stayed on; that he was dead before he hit the floor and gone before you opened the door? Isn't that how the song goes? Doesn't matter.

What does is what he did; what Bobby *chose* to do—how he opened my eyes. I see this now, as I have been saying—all of it; what life is *really* all about; this great and secret show. I think I'm going to try and find God now. I think I need to. Not that I have been back-tracking, but these last few months, well…they have been stressful. With the facility change as well as the new medication you have me on.

All I want to do is help. That's all I *need.* I have to make up for everything that was before, everything *I* was before—this is what Bobby gave me, what he cut from me in pounds; that to sacrifice is selfless, and more than holding doors. We are here for a *reason.* It has been glimpsed, now it must be shown. Bobby, he put me on the path—you must let me ride.

#THEMEDIUMISTHEMESSAGE

I've lined them up, positioning them five feet apart as I go. As I am far from what you'd call strong, this took some doing, but once we find ourselves at the end I'm confident the message I'm trying to send will be clear to the audience it seeks.

My name is Neena Koufax. I do this of my own free will.

The medium I have chosen for today is a unique one. I don't want to spoil any of the mechanics involved, not quite yet, so instead I'll just say the situation Caldeen University has come to be in is unique as well, so in the spirit of calling a spade a spade, I believe we'll label things a wash.

Long story short: fourteen Caldeen University dental students were accused of participating in a Facebook group that joked about drugging and then raping their classmates. An external investigation was launched as complaints arose in regards to the university's bungling of its own initial investigation. One step better: the university refused to identify the students it suspended. By suspend they referred to the clinical practice setting as opposed to the classroom setting.

Bullshit, all of it, and only because I'm living proof.

"You wanna come by tonight? Bring Rhonda if you can." That was how it began, there with an invite. Rhonda couldn't go though, and eventually it had been me and three other third-year students who showed up the time it happened to me. The gas they used was the stuff from class, the stuff we would eventually use on the patients we would come to care for. The only caring going on the night before I woke up a changed woman was of the selfish kind.

These are evil men you have before you; vulgar. Every goddamn one.

Complaints filed, investigation begun, I feel defeated, demoralized, as though everything is slipping away; that the men who raped me and posted about it "in jest" are being allowed to continue their education even though they laugh as if destroying me wasn't a big thing. Only when the university herds them together does my mind turn to a more basic mode, a baser level.

You know what? I believe I need to pause here for a moment, for me to just let you in on some things before we continue on. I won't take too long here, not if I can help it. Before switching to dentistry, I was *in it for the glory* is what I want to tell you all: surgeon all the way. Things change though, plans are adapted, and sometimes you just fall in love with something more than you ever thought possible. Know what I mean? This is how I came to Caldeen University. The background I give is for later in the show, before the plunge, when you might require knowledge as to how I've kept them alive for as long as I have. Just a heads up is what I guess this is then, that and nothing more.

I realize I won't be getting away with this either, but really, this is not the point I'm trying to make. What is is this: there are consequences to our actions. Always has been, always will be. Some will get away with things. Others will not. It's the way this world of ours works. Perhaps things need to change then, yes? And that's where this began, when that little voice inside my head decided to take a trip. I understood that if I didn't stand up for myself they would never get what they deserved. Oh they'd get something alright, a little bit for sure, but would it be just when compared to what each of them put all nine of us through?

No is the answer you're looking for.

And if you can't find it in yourself to think this way then God have mercy you never run into someone like me.

Oh, you hear that? Someone's waking up! C'mon, let's go see. Lots of stairs, I know, but at least the room has remained secure. I filled it with the same gas they used on me; put it out slow as class was being taught. Professor Burston has been affected by this as well and you can see him over there, asleep behind his desk. Just so we're clear, he has not been harmed in the making of this.

Okay. Almost there. As I've said, once I realized where they had been placed and that all of them would be together at the same time is when the shit got real. I mean, let's face it—it was like a dream come true. One born of a nightmare, sure, but you get what I'm saying. Once I saw the place…I mean, look at it! How high up they are, how circular it is, each of them leaning down from the guard rail they've been tethered to. And that the room is technically a circle is a boon unto itself, each position channeled back toward my live feed at the center. Refurbished, it's an old school teaching space, one the university takes pride in, full of staggered seating and standing room only around the top. This is a good thing. No, it's more than a good thing—it's apt. You know why? Because it's old school justice I'm about to hand out.

Oh, it's Jackson! And of course it is! Hey there, bud. A little groggy are you? Yeah, it's to be expected. No, no, don't try and pull yourself free. Not till you take a good look at what I've used to tie you to the rail. Look down, c'mon, don't be such a sorry sport! Didn't stop you when you had me down, did it? "Hate sex" is what you call it, no? What you posted? You also say the penis is a tool for men to teach women all they need to know. Those were your words, weren't they? The ones I'm pulling up now? I know. I know. The tape *is* rather tight but just go ahead and give us a nod then. There, see, not so bad. No smiles now though, eh? Not for this camera, no. For the others sure, yeah, why not, no one is going to really do anything about a bunch of girls who can't even remember the night in question, are they? That was another one of yours I think. Or maybe that was Mark. What say you, Mark? Yes, Mark, I know you're awake. We all do; there is a camera pointed at each of you. I imagine we're ready then? No one needs an explanation as to why we are here, do they? Fellas, c'mon! Tears, really? I mean, really-truly? Okay. Okay. Since this whole thing began with a question I'll end it with one: within the abdominal cavity of the average male how much intestine do you think he carries? Anyone? The small intestine is about twenty feet in length and the large is five. Since I'm using both we'll add them together. Twenty-five feet times fourteen of you is... okay...let's see, carry the one. Wow! That's three hundred fifty feet of you! Or as I like to say: one hundred five meters of hanging entrails in response to the penetration of nine women who never gave consent. It equals what the boys and girls at home have already figured out. What? Some of you fellas still look confused. Fine. I can take care of that. You ready then? Okay. Here goes. Contrary to what people believe, it's the destination that things are about, not the journey. Two, it will be the large intestine going first. And third? Well third is what this exercise has been about; what your penises have gone and taught.

Safe travels, boys. Enjoy the fucking trip.

LOVE, IT MAKES THE WORLD GO ROUND

I'd like to say it was my earliest memory that I knew I was different. Not the case. Add about four years to the total and then I knew something was up. Follow this with the cats I graduated to and yeah, I'm thinking running over a family of toads with the lawnmower and realizing I didn't give a shit is when my tendencies went and made themselves known.

You understand what it is I'm saying here? It's importance?

Good. Wouldn't want anything getting lost in the translation.

So I do the cats. Make my way to dogs. And then come about seventeen I go live, become a big game hunter, and say my whatnots to old Mr. Kemper who lived two farms down. Did a number on that man too, his bib overalls the same color of his shirt by time the thresher catches bone. Unfortunate accident they said. Bad things just sometimes happen to good people. You don't say.

I'm never suspected. Never even asked. Weird, I know, but by this time I'd already figured out how to play the game. Have been playing it my entire life now that I mention it. Fifty-some-odd years and not even so much as a sniff. Means I'm doing something right. Means I might be smarter than your average bear. Might also mean my time is coming and I'm only as lucky as the next guy. This seems more likely the case, as I'm a firm believer in the law of averages.

But I'm having fun. Oh yes. Loads. Which brings us to you and how you fail to see things as you should.

Molly. Molly-Molly-Molly.

The way Rob treats you is not the way a person should be treated. Not someone such as you. You are a fine woman, strong and opinionated. Your hair is long and your eyes are bright. But I know this is just for show. Parts of it anyway. I can respect that. I have to. Not because I have seen the medication your doctor has you on but because sometimes we all need a little alone time to let out the air.

It's okay, I'm on your side.

And you never asked for help, correct, but I am a man who not only believes in averages but one who is compelled to do what he thinks is right whenever he can. This might run counter to what the world thinks of men like me but it is who I am regardless. Just because you did not give me a key and I had one made does not make me any less forthright than the next guy. I'm only look-ing out for you, ensuring you are as safe as can be. It's why I friended you on Facebook and joined all the groups you like. I also "happened" upon your pass-words, doing so from my computer late at night. You are quite the little saver I see, though you do still owe quite a bit on your student loan. This here, us getting to know one another, this is what eventually leads me to your underwear drawer and why I eventually try on all nineteen pairs. We have touched now, you and I, but not as I want, nor as I need. It's why I find your dirty clothes bin and pull out the final two pairs. You are on them, in them, and then so am I. As I knew you would be, you are exquisite. It's why Rob will never again touch you as he'd like, why you will never again wear nothing but turtlenecks for weeks.

You understand what it is I'm saying here? It's importance?

I am not as stupid as I look, not when it comes to matters concerning the heart. Some are, sure, and this is the reason I took our Rob home to the old farm where my dearly departed parents eventually purchased old Mr. Kemper's thresher. As is its purpose, the big machine eats, the time between sittings quite vast indeed. I want to say Rob understood this but the man seemed a little preoccupied there at the end. Some could wonder why.

It means you are safe now. Or safer than you were. I will continue to check in on you from time to time. I might even say hi. If I do, a word of caution. Do not ignore me, not as you have. Not after everything I've done. Give credit where credit is due. At least do that. It would also help for you to remember and believe in what makes this world go round.

If anything, I would have you do that.

MORE THAN THEY COULD KNOW
To be fair, I think I have always been like this

Cycling down, compressing, I watch as the arms and legs hanging outside the machine snap off like muted branches. Thick and bleeding, they fall to the concrete floor, no longer a part of what once made them whole. Occasionally—perhaps one in five—these appendages roll toward me, but most times they do not. Inert, they remain still about my feet, each piece a rearranged fragment of something which will never again be.

It is Sunday, pre-church, and before the morning rush.

Did I care that they made fun of me? Yes. More than they would ever know. Did I show it? Never, not once. I am good at things like this, at holding them in. I let them stew, boil. It's how I've come to cook; how the man inside me rolls. In the mirror, naked, I repeat: *I am Rage.*

At seventeen I was hit by a car. Scars come, many, and to this day still I limp because of it. My right hand turns inward as well, up and toward my chest. It resembles a claw, but one which has lost the will to live. I'd like to say chicks dig this, but no, this has never been the case.

Mr. Gray, the manager at Mister Food, keeps me on

staff even though corporate had suggested otherwise. I give the man credit for that. I truly do even though I have been told this more times than I care to count. Mr. Gray—he of the tall, the bald, and the very bad breath— shouldn't have done what he did though, and only because of what it produced. Truth be told, he should of given me severance; just ensured I went away. He didn't, however, and soon after is when I find out that Mr. Gray is no better than all the others talking behind my back. Mr. Gray never yells at me, nothing as vulgar as that. But he whispers along with the rest of them, and at times I have seen him laugh.

It is this which has caused me to do the things I've done.

Why I rage. Why I seethe. Why I formed big bad habits.

The final straw is the baler, and the day that Mr. Gray takes me aside. He tells me the machine is only meant to house cardboard and plastic, that only a bale of each could be made at a time. I say I understand this; that it hadn't been me who'd mixed the two. It's here that Mr. Gray chooses to call me a liar, and his voice, had it been raised? I can't recall, not really. What I do see is my fellow employees and how they have stopped dead in their tracks, there to glare and stare. One of them had been Sara, a girl I had at one time wished to call my own. She would never fuck me though, and I have never held any delusions concerning that.

"And, Ronald, seriously, you need to be washing your uniform more than once a week." I nod, take what has been given, and then watch as Mr. Gray begins to walk away. From the side I see him roll his eyes as he passes Patrick, Bill, and Mark. They smile in turn, the secret shared and understood. The rage comes forward then, leaping, but I smash it down, my wide and toothy grin fighting to contain that which no longer wanted to be contained. This is a skill, something I'd come to excel at, the fuel which has filled me these last few years.

It's only later that the staff meeting at the end of the month goes and enters my mind.

They are always held on Sundays, before store opening, and out back where Mister Food keeps all of its excess stock. Mr. Gray rents folding chairs and everyone gets a seat. To the right, beside these seats, looms the baler. Industrial grade and painted brown, it possesses a mouth I had come to dream of: six feet long, three feet wide, and five feet deep. Plastic and cardboard, Mr. Gray had said, saying it as though I were someone new.

Producing rectangle kids, you fed the baler until you no longer could. Full, you pressed the button which activated the plunger, three thousand pounds of pressure then compacting recyclables the only way it could. Needless to say, I was far from wondering about cardboard and plastic as I spasmed into my hand. I was thinking about bodies; about stacking them high. Could be done, I thought, and suddenly realized I had asked the question aloud.

"Mr. Gray?"

"What is it now, Ronald?"

"At the staff meeting, if it's not too much trouble...I

was wondering…would it be okay if I was in charge of refreshments?" Pausing, Mr. Gray finally swivels in his chair. He is elated, I see, just as I thought he'd be. All told, it's shit like this that makes me want to heave. Fact is, it proves what I'd come to understand, that people like Mr. Gray don't just call the kettle black, they fucking well paint it.

The dosage I drum up is enough, more than, and all but Florence has taken a glass. It doesn't take much to persuade her, however, not once I put the full force of my limp on display. She takes the glass, sips, comments on how peachy it tastes. Thirty minutes later all thirty-seven employees lay prone before me. Where to begin, I think, and suddenly notice how hard it has become to breathe; how hard my heart is now knocking inside my chest. "I am Rage," I say and take each of them in one at a time. I will be stacking you, I think, and then go on toward Mr. Gray. In time—stupid fucking hand—I get the big man up, rolling him up and over the baler's top lip. Easier, I take the cashiers next, each of them half the weight of Mr. Gray. Eleven of them inside, I close the safety gate and then push the big green button on the side of the machine. With a start and then a screech the plunger descends, crushing bone and breath alike. They never wake, not one of them. They only bleed, forming a lake like the syrup we kept in aisle nine.

The buggie boys come next, followed by the ladies who ran Floral. Of them all, it's Sheila the office girl who proves the most difficult. Over three hundred pounds, she is more than I can lift. Using empty milk crates, I stack them like steps and create the leverage I believe I will need. In, she sinks halfway down, her face coming to rest next to George from Frozen Food. Amanda is beside them, her brain exposed and grey.

Finished, I look around at the empty chairs, at the skids full of overstock and beyond. I take in the blood that continues to seep from the bottom of the baler and the arms and legs that rest within. Should I leave them, I think, but realize I have been trained too well; that a job is not complete until you have cleaned up after yourself. Smiling, I make a bale using twine that will never again be white. It does not turn out as I hoped, not as rectangular, nor as solidly built.

From skin that runs in flaps to muscle that hangs and drips, I stand in front of the baler's open door, squint into the chamber for all the faces I can still make out. There in the corner is Stacy and Beth, both of them covered in what remained of Stu. Below them I see Richard, the man finally making his way inside Peggy-Sue. And there at the bottom lay Mr. Gray, his bright eyes now dull, his nose beneath his mouth.

To reiterate: Did I care that they made fun of me? Yes.

More than they could know.

I REMEMBER

I remember holding you in my arms for the first time. How you turned your head and grasped my finger with yours. It's how I fell in love.

You had blue eyes at first and eyelashes as long as your mother's even though you weren't an hour old. I remember feeding you, bathing you, and pretending to hurt myself because of how it made you laugh. All told, the very best parts of any parent's day.

I remember walking you to school. Pre-school. Kindergarten. All the grades up to and including four. You are ferocious in your learning, hungry for everything that was new. I remember figure skating, Minx the cat, and all the times I carried you to bed. The teeth you lost and the smiles you gave; a heart which seemed to dance. All of it, every part: our lives as meant to be.

I remember the officers, their posture, and how they held their hats as they stand outside our door; that our prearranged meeting time for walking home alone had come and gone and the grace period you knew nothing about had come and gone as well. This is how it starts. How we knew something had gone wrong. Once he has been caught, I tried my best to burn holes into the back of what passes for his head. He never turns to meet me, not in all the years it takes.

I study him, dream of him, and become something less in the exchange, a version of myself I can't help but begin to hate. Your mother tries with me, cries with me, but everything you were is bigger than the sun. I give her what she wants, but not what I believe she needs.

I fall further, deeper, the blackouts I create as feared as they are embraced. I want oblivion. I want clarity. Each and neither at the very same time. Only when I'm told he's been granted early release am I able to put these things away. Not for me, but for you, because you were my child.

Free, I remember the day he is paroled and the day I follow him back to his father's farm. He bolts when he sees me, recognition creating flight. I pass goats and cows and un-mucked stalls as my body becomes younger than it is, faster than it should be. Unlike him, this comes from memory. From days I longed to know.

I follow him up the silo, his face turned down toward mine. It's exactly as I picture your face, there when your fear was at its worst. At the top I stop, step forward, my mind ablaze and set. He knows this, sees this, his mouth going on and on and on. I don't think, only act, and ensure I end up on top. We fall, him screaming, my hold upon his body stronger than the stone atop your grave. It compresses when we hit, collapses, crushing breath and bone alike. Liquid splashes upwards, outwards. I feel it mix with mine.

I recall all of this, every bit, but the part I remember

most is how I held you in my arms. How you turned your head and grasped my finger with yours.

It's how I fell in love.

THE PLACE BEFORE THE PLACE

Wincing, you prepare, and as the car swerves hard onto the pavement, your back is jabbed by the pointy end of the tire iron which is wedged and leaning at an improbable angle. It's not the first time this has happened. Cursing, you can only hope the driver will ensure it is the last.

In the dark you struggle to free your hands against the duct tape they have wrapped around the wrists you find behind your back. It never gives, not an inch, but still you believe the strength will come. Drenched, your hair falls into your eyes, lays matted to your forehead. It's hot in here, a furnace, but you know the majority of the heat is more from you and the situation you have gotten yourself into; that this, the trunk, is no more than the place before the place.

You swallow, spit, your breathing unlike anything you have experienced before. Not from playing ball, from running, or even from sex. This is breathing scared. Or perhaps you're hyperventilating and you just don't know the difference. Either way, it was stupid what you did, skimming. Did you think they wouldn't catch on? Better yet, did you have to up the stakes? In what world

THE PLACE BEFORE THE PLACE

is an extra five grand a month considered chump
change?

You shake your head, unable to answer your own
questions. Instead you think of Luke, of how he will
continue life without a father; that you will never get to
teach him all the things never taught to you. You well up
at this, there in the dark, and just once you wish you
were able to remember the face of your own father; a
glimpse, a flash, a smile. Next you envision Becka, she
within your arms, and at one moment she is naked, in
another she is not. *It will be the end of us*, you hear her
proclaim, and deep down you have always known her to
be right. The type of life you chose far from what your
dreams had been. However, there can be no blame, not
upon anyone who is not you. A man grown, choice becomes our own, each one dying and alive at the very
same time, this very moment proving your entire point.
You didn't have to get in Big Mike's car that day; neither
did you have to agree with what he asked of you.
Opposing him would have provoked a beating, sure, and
let's face it, possibly your life for simply saying no. But
the choice would have been better than what you do
years later, believing you deserved a little something
more in addition to what the man was paying.

There in the dark you think of these things, the story
which has become your life. You see things fast, a blur,
but you also see them slow. In one you are six and crying, fallen from your bike. Suddenly your mother appears and like always the pain is run away. She holds
you and hugs you and whispers that things will be

alright. You believe her, hold her, and why the hell would you not? She is your mother, your life, and not for the majority of your time together passed out on the floor. She never hits you, not often, but when she does it's accompanied by regret. A chaser we'll call it, and only after the bottle is done.

Suddenly the car begins to slow. You hear gravel and pavement and then gravel once more. Slower now, you can make out the voices of the men inside the car but not the words they speak. Do you really need to know what they are saying? No, you don't think you do. The sudden warmth spreading about your groin tells you everything you need to know. Stopped, all four doors open and gravel comes underfoot. Like it's nothing, you can hear them now, each of them shooting the shit like they don't have a care in the world. Benny and Bob go on about the Bucks, Carlos and Stacks smoking and nodding their heads in agreement.

Is this really happening, you think, and realize that you have been straining so hard that something lets go in your head, a pop. It's small, not painful, and somehow feels like the color red. You begin to scream and scream and thrash about the trunk. You hear laughter, more, and then one of them kicks the side of the car and tells you to knock the shit off. You fail to comply, which of course only speeds the process up.

They open the trunk, freedom, and you erupt up-wards as the fresh air rocks you. The taste is sweet, like butter, and oh so better than wine. You fall forward, belched from the trunk, the dirtiest tongue alive. Halfway down, as your face and gravel meet, you, the middle of you, is caught by the hitch. You groan, go fetal, and all you hear is laughter as you writhe and take the pain. You squint, tell them to fuck right off, and then take notice of the stars, that there are none, that it is only the moon which lights the way.

One of them, Bob you think, pulls you up, throws you back down. "Shunta did what ya done, Ricky," he says and then spits into your face. The saliva is hot and gross and you picture rotting meat as it slides into your mouth. Inside, it makes you want to run as far and fast as you possibly can. Instead you scream and shake your head as violently as your neck allows. A second later, before you see them, you feel the wood; all four, and then your screams begin anew. They beat you, break you, crush you. Swing after swing after swing. Jagged and loose, your bones are transformed, like powder that has run to soup; all bones, to every appendage and ex-tremity you own. Skin is next, gone, removed and replaced by a pulp that now exists—and still you are aware! How, you think, and understand the stupidity of your question the moment it is asked: to ensure every effort is taken in making you feel everything that comes before.

The choice is obvious, befitting your crime, as you know how the men above you work; have done the job yourself, in fact. Bleeding, dying, you watch the end draw near. Down, the bats obliterate your mouth, your nose and the top of your skull. Last, they save your eyes and the truth each one has struggled to hide. Unrecognizable, you heave and spurt, your gurgling breath the only sound into the night. You think of Luke and Becka and your mother during the times that she is real, her love sober. As the final arc comes down and takes it all apart you can only wonder: Was this really all I am?

SAVING THE WORLD,
ONE APPLIANCE AT A TIME

"Can you hear me now?"

I know. I know. But we only get the one go round, right?

We're at the place, our special place, and my work face has replaced my everyday face, lack of hair included. "I'm only going to tell you why they call me 'The Arm' once. Do yourself a favor: listen the fuck up and slow the fuck down. You do that, all three of us can get to the places each of us needs to be." I look over to Randy, offer him the megaphone. He shakes his head, pulls his pants up and over his ever expanding gut. "I ever once take that thing when you ask?"

I smile and look back down toward the man of the hour; to the man whose name is Paul. He's wearing skinny jeans and a ratty flannel shirt which flails each time he tries to run up the sides of the pool. Sliding back down, nothing changes, the man coming to rest within beers cans, wines bottles, and other, less distinguishable waste. "It was an accident, really, me getting that nick-name. Me and my brother here just doing our bit the day it went down," I go on, my voice twenty-six stories high.

I tell him of Marty Barnes and how he and that particular piece of shit shared the same strain of dirtbag; middlemen to monsters who used children like toys. Taken by surprise, Barnes gets past both Randy and I that day but Randy, his abdomen nowhere near the unstoppable expansion it will become, is up and after him before I can pull myself from the floor. Dazed, I hit the balcony in hopes of becoming a lookout.

"Everything happens fast after that. I mean, really fast."

In boxers and a beater-T, Barnes is below me, twenty stories down and catching his breath behind a rusted-out Ford. To my left, on the concrete, is the air conditioner I would become famous for. I pick it up, heave, and call out to Barnes two or three seconds after the leaking machine has left my hands. Now, I have never been the best of shots, not on the best of days, but I will admit to being somewhat lucky in life. It's the only reason Barnes takes off when he does I think, and why he looks up and back the moment I call his name. "I saw his eyes too, there before the metal took each of them away. Not fun. Not how you'd think. Every last bit of bone, hair, and grey matter parceled out into something like a nine-foot radius. This doesn't even include the blood puddle his neck creates."

My little speech done, I release the bowling ball I'd been taunting in promise. Lob it like the weapon of destruction I want it to become. The man screams as it descends. Continues to scream as the concrete above his head cracks, relents, and comes to hold the ball like an eye. Behind me, Randy sighs. "You know you have a problem, right?"

I want to ignore him, I do, but sometimes a brother is the only friend a man can have. "It's only a problem if you can't stop. I've read the books. Pretty sure you should read them too." He eyeballs me hard, just like our father used to do. It doesn't do half of what he thinks it does but it's a game neither of us can quit. Not if we wanted answers.

I turn back round, drop ball after cinderblock after microwave oven. The balls I found on sale at SPORT-CHEK, everything else being me adjusting to the environment I'd been given. So you know, either way.

The man named Paul dances and rolls, shucks and jives, and still I come close to hitting him more times than not. I can't quite hear the words pouring from his mouth, not really, but a pretty good bet would be he knew we were done with fucking about.

Last bowling ball deployed, I straighten first my holster and then my badge. Randy does the same.

Time to see if our incentive took.

Time to see if our bird was ready to sing.

THE STRUGGLE IS REAL

New plan: find a better class of man.

This is what's going on under my extensions as Renee's "friend" levels his gun at my head. Well okay, there's a little bit more to it than that, I suppose, but stuff such as this is meant to come with the territory, no? Instead I have what I have: my sixteenth failed relationship in as many goddamn years.

Man had a handle too, which maybe-kinda-sorta should have been a tip-off right out of the gate. Me and judgement though, we tend to pretend we understand one another right up until the bruises appear, the money runs out, or the dope and drink start quenching things better than I have ever been able to.

Brings us to Renee, the newest guy in my life. A Frenchman, I still recall his smile when we met, his big hairy hands over mine. *Hey, you would like to dance?* he says with his mouth. His eyes are a whole other story. Finding Dory, perhaps. But rebooted. The end result coming to hold not just one type of shark, but the whole damn species.

Okay, those eyes said, *but first I'm gonna go on and*

eat you up. And you know what? You are going to enjoy the way I chew.

So yeah, I'd known from the get-go I might have been out of my depth. Sure, I like to fool myself as much as the next person and really, who doesn't? But there comes a time. Christ, does there.

"No hands. Just suck." A tall order, sure, but one I have always been game for. Oh yes. Every inch of the way. Not because the performance is a particular thing of mine, but because I am a people pleaser to my core. Might be because daddy touched me I'm like this. Might be because my mother did not. Either way, it comes down to a combination of loneliness, gentlemen callers, and bad decision making so epic, statue, honor, and erected should be the only names I respond to. Doesn't help I like to be fucked often and well either, but even that right there is me stretching things somewhat. I need to always be with someone I suppose. For the majority of time I'm awake and breathing I mean. Gets me into trouble is what this does, and mixed up with guys one rung below the bar of standards methinks.

Brings us to the fridge full of body parts Renee and I end up staring into. "Well, pet, would you look at this?" He didn't have to say it. Not in the least. My eyes just about outta my goddamn skull. We'd already found what we'd come for: the dope. What I was told was in lieu of a payment owed. Renee's "friend," our "ower," some sorta Richie Rich-type. Chandeliers and paintings the whole place over. Stairs and sofas and rugs so plush I could more or less swim. Why the hell didn't we leave when we had the chance then? Why make our way to the lower level and the red/black curtains we should have never pulled back?

"Just want to take a peek around, pet. Won't be but a tic." But it was a tic. Many tics. Arms and legs. Torsos and thighs. Wasn't the worst of it though. Not by a country fucking mile.

Turning, I feel the heat of the bullet that enters the back of Renee's head go past the bridge of my nose like breath coming from God. My man's chest hair and skinny jeans fly forward in response, what remains of his head slamming into a crisper full of ring fingers and thumbs. I scream. Go to my knees with my hands held tight against my ears. Takes me a few seconds but I begin to realize I'm still alive. I look up, unable to control my shaking, my eyes right into the bright blue of the dude holding the gun. He's older than Renee, darker, and the man-bun he's attempting has just about come undone.

"You here by choice or did that piece of shit force you?"

There are many things I could have said. Many things I could have done. Wishing to remain whole, I recount my life as best I can. Done, he says, "That so? If it is, prove it."

I rise. Wipe my face. Tuck my hair. Take hold of the axe he motions to, the one hanging just back from the side of the fridge. I dig in and swing, the power I unleash into what remained of Renee something I never knew I had. It's cathartic, primal, and I scream the entire time it takes to take his body apart.

"See?" I say, and my breath comes out of me as it does after sex.

He says he does, yes, and then he lowers the gun. I seem to see him for the first time as he does this, and the exchange that comes scares me more than what I have just been through.

It is the look of lust which stares back at me. The look of love.

Fuck—just my type.

DARNELL
(WAITING ON THE DAY)

I watch from up high; me, the king of building nine. This is what I tell myself, wearing shorts I've yet to change. The rifle is beside me, like a pet whose silence is learned. In the lawn chair I sit, a man now forty-five. Bone-thin, wiry, I eat Fritos until the bag is done. I chase the chips with a single Bud and then another because I can. Passing the fridge I see my unshaven face, look past my lying eyes. I think, *Why do you go on*, but the thought is fleeting, gone and replaced faster than it is made. Things are easier this way, when delusion is at its peak.

Back on the balcony, back in my chair, I further my vigil still, somewhat giving what I got. Does that make sense? Not really. Do I care? Not one fucking bit. What intrigues me is the day; the journey it might provide. It gives me hope, as it always has, ever since this thing I do began. To the east the day begins, peaking, and then runs every way at once. Shadows stretch, traffic comes; with traffic, people, and people, bikes. Some run, most walk, but ever onwards each of them march. On and on they ride, unaware it's all a lie. Or perhaps they know the truth, and like me, wish for something more. Bull-

103

shit, really, but a flavor made popular by what passes for the times.

Across from me are apartments, more buildings, the hospital and church. Factories are in the background, history to the land. Here I watch a man openly drunk at a quarter past ten. I focus on him tight, the sight above my gun giving me a clear and present pose. Paper bag in hand, dressed in unkempt clothes and a red fedora hat, he weaves in front of the Drug-Mart, happy as a lark. He is singing it seems, or quite possibly conversing with himself. Women walk by him, and men, patrons, each veering as if he were contagious. Perhaps he is, and the fear they have is justified. I would question it however, believing the fear portrayed a shame. They know his look, his truth; that too easily the same could happen to them.

Last week, one block over, a man and woman fought behind their car where their drive and the sidewalk meet. He wore a muscle-T, she a too-tight dress. Her hair was red and his shaved bald. Once he hit her, then twice, and she crumbled to the ground. He does a dance of some sort, like he's proud, and I fixate on his pants, that they hang too fucking low. Suddenly another man appeared; he who intervenes. He is black and wearing a blue bandana and is bigger than the man he confronts. They duel verbally, face-off, and then the shit gets real. Baldy pulls a knife and cuts Bandana deep. From my sight I see it bloom, his shirt a violent mess. But Bandana is far from done, and to my surprise he kicks the first man's legs out from under him. As ground and Baldy meet I hear the sirens first faint, then loud, then watch as they approach. One car, two cops, and Bandana has his hands raised even before the cops are out of the black and white. Baldy is not as smart. The big cop takes him down, a Taser before his rights; a knee as well, there in the middle of his back as both officers applied the glinting cuffs. The man who intervened, he is the one I was meant to see, the reason I carry on.

The day continues, hot, and I forget about the fight. I concentrate on today, wonder if I'll be around come this time tonight. I change my view, then again, and then another time after that. I am looking, you see, watching, in anticipation of a glimpse.

To my left I see him, soft and dull and thick. His brown hair screams of murder, of the secret self within. A duffle bag is over his right shoulder, held by meaty mitts. The bag is big and black and I believe it contains a head. It's there in the way he walks, alive in the color of his jeans. I follow him through my scope, letting the nose of the gun rest upon the balcony's old and rusted rail. His step is brisk, his loafers light, and I hold the gun tighter than I ever have before. One little squeeze, I tell myself—all it would take and the monster would cease to exist.

The air conditioner surges, gurgles, and I turn my head to look. The back of it drips as it has always done and my thoughts, they change again. I stub my toe on the bottom of the barbeque as I go to get another beer and sleeve of white saltines. The crackers I eat at once, and only because I'm never full. Clean your plate. Mind your mom. Do what's told is right. These are the things that make me who I am. At least that's what I've been told. I don't know, though. It seems to me there is another man, a future self, and he is only tucked away. He is the man who screams inside our eyes when the world is beyond our grasp. He is dark, this man, but seldom is he heard. Seen, yes, and only because of what he sells. "I have paid my dues," I say aloud and resume the day that's come.

No longer gone, the woman from the corner of Park is clean and ready to work. She presents herself, finds a john, and I follow them as I can. In his car she gets to work and I envision Halle Berry, more specifically, one of the many characters she has played. The john is no Sam Jackson, the opposite in fact; white and fat and bald, pasty as an un-popped zit. She works him though, full bore, and soon the transaction is complete.

In front of the Drug-Mart, I check in on the drunk; the man continues his dance. Cars drive in and cars drive out. Out loud I recite each of their license plates and then aim for every head. I get them all, every shot, and predict how it goes down. They stand as I shoot, the first shot locking them in place. A moment later a woman screams, her scream becoming the dam. Breaking, they run, each of them searching but unsecure. I pick them off as they go, as many as I can; one down, two, each in the back of the head. Panic reigns, faces explode, flotsam to the wind—

Brakes lock, lock hard, and the familiar screech begins. There is time however, and the driver, male, avoids what could have been a very costly mess. I sit back, lay the gun across my lap. It is fine wood, a stock barrel, and I caress it like a pet. A present from my father, I have never felt it spent. I dream of it happening, I do, on days quite like today. It never comes to pass. Not as I would like. This is where God comes in; where he goes and rights the day. They say to temper evil there must always come some good. He's good like that, at messing with my head. If ever there was a secret man.

In the parking lot the car is moving much too fast. The girl is small, away from her mother's eye, and I see this all without my scope. The drunk does too, and as she walks down from the curb he is after her faster than I would have thought. In seconds the car will strike her, kill her, as I know it's supposed to do. It does not however, and the man's fedora is given flight instead. Sacrifice they will say, and that the man had been a hero every single day. They will say this with pride and wear it like joy, each of them forgetting how they would come to stand clear of him not a week past from the day. This is human nature though, the beast who loves and attacks. For forty years I have known this, since my father gave me sight.

"Darnell?" she says, and I know at that moment that my day has come undone. Dead drunk or not, when Petra calls, I am there to answer.

I find her by the door, grocery bags in hand. "You just gonna stand there? C'mon, help a woman out." I do. I take the bags and put away my other self, the one from deep inside. It is time to form my face for her, the one she needs to see.

"Something's going on outside, over at the 'Mart. Lots a screaming and carrying on as I drove by. You seen it, I suppose?"

"Looks like a man died," I say, and she stops so suddenly I think I've left my other self out for her to see.

"You don't got that gun out there again, do you?"

"Petra, dear; is that the type of man I am?"

"I don't know," she says, and lumbers toward the dining room table. She fits, barely, and I watch as her body forms to the shape of the chair. For better or worse, I said, on the very same day as she. "It's just when a man, when he starts to spend most of his days on a balcony with a gun, it tends to make a woman nervous."

I smile softly as she says this, believing it conveys everything I wish to say. In the kitchen I find her treat jar half full, at just below the line she never likes to see. I take it to her, remove the lid. Standing, I feed her peanut butter cups, one and then another. She accepts them gratefully, her breath now fuller than before. Upon her fifth she pulls me close. Tight, she holds me around the waist, whispers that all she does is worry. I tell her that there isn't need, that today has come and gone—but then I feel myself stir. Petra does too, and soon I am home within her face. She doesn't mind, and hasn't since the scale could no longer take her weight. Not that I do either, as her mouth is just as warm.

"I am only looking for a glimpse, Petra, all I've ever

asked, that the evil of this world is being held at bay." I tell her this, knowing it is exactly what she needs, that for Petra it is more about right than it is about wrong. It is a fallacy, of course, but the blinders are the armor my wife has always had to wear. Nodding, she continues her pace; slow, but full, all in. She cares, she does, and the peanut butter smell is nice. What I don't explain is that the chamber is never empty and that tomorrow could very well be the day. Done, I take her chin in my hand and thank her for my gift. Shorts up, I give her the grin that she requires, the one that says I am who I should be, and then I go for the remote. "Come on!" I say. "I think *Jeopardy* might still be on."

REGRETS? I'M THINKIN' YEAH

Two days before I die Michael is hip deep in me from behind. I understand why this has entered my mind so I might as well go one better and say I've always liked sex this way, soon as I realized there was an actual choice as to how the act could be performed. It was the same thing with deep throating; a class I mastered my sophomore year. I'd like to say these things are inconsequential, but I can't, not after I realized it had been Linda who'd hit me from behind.

Heavy set, with all the fat pooling in places woman do not like, Linda would be Michael's wife of twenty-two years. I would like to say something nice about this woman, seeing as it was me fucking her husband, but no, I can't, and I pretty much have to go and blame the noose around my neck as to the reason why. It doesn't stop me from using my big girl voice to scream *bitch* as loud as I can. Cunt comes into play as well, but that too remains inside, there behind whatever type of gag she has jammed inside my mouth.

"He always said he didn't want children. The love he had, he said it was only enough for me. Both of us know better than that though, don't we?" I can't even say she is talking to me. Oh she is, don't get me wrong, but the woman's demeanor is distracted, her appearance disheveled and, boy howdy, was she willing to pace. Back and forth, cigarette after cigarette, she is on about my body, my tits, and the tightness of my ass. Yoga pants. Sport bras. The things I probably let Michael do in the soft dark hole of my mouth. Yeah, feels like she'd been saving that last one.

"What is a woman to do," she says. "How is one expected to compete?" I understand all this, every part. But I also don't care, not as I should. Reasonable? Depends on how you look at things. I am in life for me and only me and I can say this no other way. Sure I could play the part of a human being as well as anyone, but only if it allowed me to acquire the things that make life worth living. Sound familiar? That's okay. I lied to myself for a long time too.

I've lied about other things as well. Many things. What I cannot run from is this defense mechanism going on inside my head right now. I mean, that has to be what's going on, right? If not, just who is it I'm talking to then?

"I guess the question I really want answered is this. Did you even consider what you could be destroying?" Would I give her the answer she wanted if I were able? Hell, if I wasn't hanging from this tree? I can't say, not with any kind of certainty. I could tell her it wasn't me who initiated. Me who said they'd be leaving their wife whether he'd met me or not. Probably not the type of disclosure a woman in Linda's condition needed to hear, but then again my options had fallen somewhere between fucked and Sunday so perhaps I should cut myself some slack.

This brings tears. Blubbering, really. The woman I had become reduced to the teenager she loathed. Not a declaration I am overly proud of, no, as I consider myself as strong as I am selfish, but things are coming to an end remember, my time left upon this world now minutes at best.

And yes, I do want to live. More than anything, yes. But the realist in me, she has always been strong.

Understanding as much as I think I do, I do what I believe she wants me to. I apologize. Doing so with the only tools left in my box: eyes which plead and beg to a mouth which grunts and groans as my body twists as best it can while balancing upon the birdbath beneath me. I am given a crash course in simmering rage for my troubles; Linda's lined face a mixture of pain and despair and hate as she comes forward and slowly removes said birdbath. She does it this way so my neck will feel everything she needs it to. I am making up this last part, unable to surmise what the woman was truly thinking, but I'm pretty sure I'm not far from the mark, not from the look in her eyes.

Woman had a plan is what I see. Woman was following through.

And oh, would you look at that. Rain.

HEAVY LEGO

Okay. So here's the deal.

Most messed up thing I ever done was cut a dude in two. This takes talent. And very steady hands. Doesn't hurt I'd hit the gym most of my life either, but that's neither here nor there. What I really need to get back to is how true my hands had to be in order to pull something like this off—that it allowed me to split the damn bastard right across the equator.

I am by no means a "good" guy, not in the clearest sense of the word, and I would never want such a thing misconstrued. I am not "bad" either, but the line I ride is fine. Drugs and addiction are the reasons for this. I will not wrap it, what I am, so take it or leave it; I couldn't really give a fuck.

"How much it is you lookin' for?" Except for his voice, Virgil was a cross between Eric La Salle and a young Ving Rhames. Dressed in grey slacks, a beater T, and enough gold so his neck would never need a gym, he was the undisputed King of Fifth and Dime.

"Twenty, yo," I say through the bars and screen. Usually I just wait there on his porch, my dick in my hand, until Virgil decides to saunter back with what I ordered. Why today played out differently, I will never know.

"Have a seat, m'man. Take a load off. All Big Daddy wants to do is talk a little." I have never trusted people who refer to themselves in the third person. This was how the big man talked though, right down to the hand gestures to his chest and the fondling of his junk.

It was dark too, and gloomy, the only real light coming in through slats in the blinds. I asked: "Where's T-J and Bench?"

"The crew's done gone, dawg. Down to Haldone's to get the place some drink. Don't mean no never mind, though—gives us the time to talk." I know. Fuck me, right? I had no choice, though, not since a particular letter of the alphabet had gotten her hooks into me.

In front of me sat a glass coffee table. Atop this table, all the things I'd come to cherish; balloons and needles, papers and spoons. Scales too, a pair of them, where I assumed Virgil weighed every ounce he'd ever thrown my way. Above us, a ceiling fan droned on, me in the high-back chair I'd been led to and Virgil on a leather couch. The axe I would come to use stared up at me from where it rested at the bottom of the table. I did not need my spider sense to tell me the reason it'd been left there. Shit like that was bread and butter to men like Virgil, where word of mouth could work like bullets. Sometimes better.

Now I think about it, I suppose it's pretty much the reason I went and arranged him the way I did.

"You like what you been gettin', Clement? You

think—" He didn't get to finish. The door behind me—the one which led to the cages I would soon find out about—blew open.

A child no older than eight stood there. He was white, this boy, pale, and in nothing but his Fruit of the Looms. Wild-eyed, screaming, he moved toward the front door with a purpose I could relate to. He did not stop once he reached the bars; no, picked himself up and ran into them again. And then one more time for good measure. I wanted to tell the kid to stop, that it was locked and to just give us a minute, but my mind doesn't work that way. Might be because my father beat me that my mind does this, might be because my mother did not. Only thing I know for certain is that you don't fuck with kids.

"What the fuck," Virgil was standing now, as was I, the both of us truly astonished by the sight of the boy and his continued attempts to flee. As they say, it is here that the shit got real.

I look at Virgil, my grill set, and you know what this mutherfucker does in turn? It ain't bake cookies, that's for sure. We fight. One black man. One brown. Drugs go flying. Needles too. And suddenly my back is through the glass coffee table. I'm cut, sure, but I'm more worried about the hands around my neck. Struggling, kicking, watching darkness seep toward me from all sides, I reach out, grasp for anything, a piece of table, syringe, carpet, anything, and then the handle of the axe is in my hand and I swing it sideways and up and the blunt end takes Virgil in the ear. It is enough to daze him. The next whack knocks him flat out.

I jump up, sucking air harder than I ever have. In the corner by the door the kid huddles, chicken-bone arms around chicken-bone knees. I tell him to stay where he is, that he's safe for the moment, and that I just have to see. Down I go, hoping that what I'm about to find is not as evil as I feared. One look at the cameras and the cages and I know I have never been more wrong.

It is here that something shifts in my head and I realize why the axe had yet to leave my hand. It surprised me, sure, but not as much as you'd think.

What shocks me more is when the kid gets in on the action and starts to help; when he grabs the top portion of Virgil by the arms and tugs forward, big chunks of the man's busted vertebrae falling out like heavy Lego. Me, I take the legs, put about twelve feet of thick ribbon between us.

"That's good, little man. It'll do." And it did. T-J and Bench listening to every word I said with eyes wide and mouths agape, taking it all in as they looked from one piece of Virgil to the other. "No more kids," I tell them; there was a new king in town.

I am by no means a good man, I tell them, nor am I bad, but I have no problem riding the line to get me what I need.

They'd be wise to remember as much.

ALMA

The piece of shit sitting in front of Alma and me was not the man who'd wronged us. Close, but not He Who Made Mommy Go Away. This one was thin, for one, and had close-kept eyes for another. Little patches of hair sprouted from his face as well, stuff which reminded me of the squiggly things my grandmother eventually grew—not really a beard at all. Struggling against the duct tape, he looks from me to Alma and back again; had actually been doing it since I took the burlap sack from his head. Led me to believe I had the right man. That he'd been released this very morning, well, that was just in case there is in fact a God.

"You gonna behave yourself, Joel? You promise me that, I remove the gag. Sound good?" Joel nods yes, slowly, like he might think his life depended on it. Each of us were where we needed to be, my basement, around a card table I knew I would never again use for cards. Quiet, patient, Alma is to my left, her hair uneven but in the best possible braid I could manage. Behind us the refrigerator kicks on and off and then goes through the entire cycle again. Mental note: must get that fixed. Above us, a lone forty-watt bulb gives us the shadow I

119

believe we require—what a man like Joel and all his kind deserve.

You still sure about this? my wife says from somewhere in the back of my mind. It's sudden, this voice, and loud, and the only place the woman I'd married now lived. That's not true of course, not really. Not once I look into the eyes of the daughter we created. Big and brown, they pool just like Arlene's. In them I see everything I've ever needed and all the things she will ever become. It is a curse, the type of parent I am now, but it is also the reason things like this needed to be done.

"Daddy?" I grasp that I've been standing there, my hands out, the gag still within the piece of shit's mouth. It is happening more often this way, me zoning out with my thoughts like this. I make another mental note: rectify this. Alma has already been through too much.

"Sorry, baby, just thinking about your mom." At this my little girl smiles, and for a moment all is again right with the world, not a hair out of place. It's as I look back to the garbage in front me that my stomach turns and I once more become something I never thought I could be.

Truth be told, there are not enough flames in hell.

Gag removed, I give him my speech, the words I have practiced. I want to know, I tell him. I must know. Just give me a reason and I will let you go. It doesn't come, what I want. But it's not really a want, not if I'm honest. It's more of a need. To know and somehow understand how another human being could do the things he'd done. "I mean, really, what is it? What excites you enough to do that to boys? I mean, seriously?" He babbles, cries, weeps and pleads. Nothing of this was new. Not one part original. Made me angry is what this did, there with Alma looking on. It's now, in this exact moment, that I realize I have given too much up, too much time, but it's then that the true monster comes out, the one who understands he has nothing left to lose.

"And you think I'm fucked up? Dude, what about you? What is this kid? Seven? Eight? You think something like this ain't gonna scar her for life? I got news for you, fuckwad. Time to get a clue!" His voice has become hard, a snarl, thick lines of vein now out upon his neck. "But if it *was* me who'd done your wife, I'd have took my time. You got that! Made sure she felt every bit of pain I could give her. I would fuck her hard and I would rip her wide! And you want to know why, right? That's your fucking question?" Feral. Vile. Little goops of spittle in the corners of his mouth. In the blink of an eye different but yet the very same. Again I paused to think of God.

"I'll tell you the fucking reason…" he barks, but the moment passes. It's not me who shuts him down though, my gun still in the back of my pants, my eyes still holding the evil in his. It's only when the eyes holding mine are gone that I look over to Alma, her .32 drawn, her hand steady.

I ask, "How did it feel this time?"

"Better," she says, and my heart fills up with something I can't yet describe. Righteousness perhaps, but even then I'm still not quite sure.

"Come on, then, let's get you to bed. I'll clean up once I've tucked you in."

"Carry me?" And it's here, as Alma holds her arms up, that I lose myself in the eyes I helped create; that I see everything I want to see and everything I need to see. I see her mother. Her father. And everything that men like the one now missing half his face will never again take away. Not if I could help it.

"Sure, baby," I say. "Sure."

MEANWHILE, BACK AT THE RANCH

I have done questionable things. Some I am proud of. Some I have chosen to never bring up again. What grinds my gears like no other is when someone takes the time to pick on a person weaker than them. A close second has become not being able to hold my water on the regular. That's something I have no control over though, so we can go and stop feeling any type of sorry you might have been starting to feel.

It's the person not treating the other the way they should this thing is about. It's just ungentlemanly in a world in need of the opposite. Don't get me wrong; if a person is any type of dick, by all means, he or she is owed what's coming to them. But if the other side of the coin is just doing it because, well, this is what I take issue with.

Brings us to Vera and her personality of late.

Younger than me by two years, Vera is the typical frail you'd find here at the Resty Acres Retirement Home. Matching her eyes is her hair, blue, and from Vera Father Time has collected the toll he takes from us all. The wrinkles are many, sure, but for Vera they come from a life lived rather than one survived.

It was her heart that stole me though, and how dear at times that woman can be. There's more, sure, but as I've said, this world is already as ungentlemanly as it needs to be. Means you don't get to know her throat game's still good. You know, even eight decades in.

"He holds me too tight, Mick. Even after I tell him to let go. Even after he makes me cry." This is what she says to me after I finally pry it loose. Of late she'd been withdrawn, somber, and nowhere near herself come popsicle time. What? It's had worse names.

She'd been referring to the new guy assigned to her floor, Marwood, he of the stained scrubs and mullet-brown hair. Pock-marked and fat, he resembled that kid from *Leave It To Beaver*, the Beav, but you know, after he'd gotten pock-marked and fat. Admitting so, Vera nods and then sends her face down toward the floor. I stop her by taking her chin in my hand and forcing her eyes back up to mine. "Nobody hurts my best girl," I say, and then we both sit down on the edge of her bed, each of us just kind of staring out the window into the common area. I want to say something profound here, that something profound was taking place, but I have never been that kind of man. I only continued to stroke her hand, her arm, realizing for perhaps the first time that I cared for this woman more than I ever thought I would. This, of course, brought rage, waking in me skills I'd long since put to bed.

It could only happen once then, this being what I told myself, as I was not as protected as I'd been in the past;

the guys I used to run either retired themselves, dead, or working for whatever schmuck now sat on top. Meant calls were to be made. Scenarios put in place. But mainly it meant Marwood was about to have his eyes opened to the consequences a man can face when behaving in ways he should not. I'm not so sure those exact words would be spoken, but I am that he'd end up seeing my point.

"You're sayin' this guy's forcing himself onto your friend?" Donnie. One of my old crew. A man who is known to get things done. Not the smartest. Not the dumbest. But loyal. All told, it's the best any of us can ask for.

"No sex. Not like that. But the fuck gets off on hurting people in other ways. Likes to hold onto them for too long. Or too hard. You see what it is I'm sayin'?"

"A pressure-man is what it sounds like. Likes to leave his mark without leavin' a mark, you know?" About summed things up, but still, I had my doubts. Nothing concrete mind you, just my gut. "Makes me think this call is going to involve more people than just you and I."

"I'm thinkin' Old Yeller. That seem doable?"

"Man's retired too, but I can't see that stopping His Rabidness. Not once he finds out it's you who's done the asking."

And all of a sudden I can hear the smile slide into Donnie's voice. "Sounds like you have something special in mind, Mick. A reduction, maybe?"

"Nothing special, no, just what's owed."

"Yeah, special it is then."

Next time I see Marwood he's as I asked for him to

be; nowhere near as tall as he'd been the month before. I sat on the edge of the bed, me and Vera both, each of us listening intently to this man dressed in a blue work shirt, blue work pants—now tapered quite nicely at the knee thank you very much—and a ratty old cap which proclaimed *Truckers Did It By The Mile.* The Beav, aka Mullet, aka Ricky Marwood, was here to offer his apologies, he said. Wanted to look us in the eyes as he was saying them, he said. "I'm sorry," he says. I nod. Vera accepts. And as the man wheels himself from the room I can't help but follow him out. I offer him my hand, both hands; to show him how much I respect what he's become. He is less now, sure, but by accepting the outcome he has opened himself up to what I have already said the world needs more of.

I mean, less *is* more, right?

He laughs at that. And then I laugh. But where my laughter ends, his continues, there as I leave him in the hall. Not until we see him wheeled out through the common area does Vera remove her teeth.

"Your just reward," she lisps.

"My best gal," I state.

A FULL, UPRIGHT
AND LOCKED POSITION

I have been many things to many people. I could take the time and name each one but I think I'd like to try something a little different seeing how we're all together as we are. By the sound of things back there in the galley, it seems some of you might already be aware as to what's going on. That's good. I think it's needed.

All told, it reminds me of my fifth grade teacher, Mr. Doring. Verbatim, he used those exact same words as he held my head in a way no adult ever should. You remember that, don't you, Mr. Doring? I suppose it's just Bill now, seeing where we're at, but I'd still like to know if you ever thought of me through the years. Hell, there could've been more you took advantage of, but I don't really care. Not anymore.

What I do care about is the man sitting next to you. If he's still there, his name's Ben Mackleford and he was my best friend up until the summer before college. This is when he and my girlfriend decided they deserved each other more than I deserved them. It's fine. It happened. And I hope that's you out there banging on the door, Tonia. I sincerely do. If not, my second choice, without a doubt, would have to be Greg Malloy. Not many people know this about old Greg, but his mean streak—it pert near matches the color of what remains of his teeth. Our time together took place in ninth grade, where I was introduced to the benefits of toilet water and the ingesting of certain flavors which often accompanied said liquid.

Quite a time we had, Greg. Yes, quite a time indeed.

Nothing compares to the rituals of Monica Porter, however. You listening, Monica? Would you like to explain how our dynamic works or should I? Long story short is Monica likes to belittle her co-workers on a daily basis. Not overtly, but in the passive aggressive ways certain flight attendants tend to perfect.

Am I doing a good enough job explaining myself, Monica? Have I enunciated enough?

Maybe you could take a moment and ask Robbie Dunn how I'm doing. He's there somewhere. I checked. Robbie's the dude who always had my back at the job I had before this one. Stand up all the way. Until he decided it was time to stand on my back and throw a certain someone under the bus for a promotion which equated to pennies a glass. It's how I ended up becoming a pilot, really, and now that we're talking about it, how this business was set in motion in the first place.

I wonder, when I speak these things, when you hear them aloud, is the recall each of you envisions as true as it should be or is there a type of denial which manifests? It's a heavy question, sure, but I state it not in search of an answer but as a means to tell you this: all of you, even the ones I have failed to mention by name, you are who have made me who I am today. Know this. Embrace it. That being said, there are two others who have just as much skin in the game as you. I couldn't get them to join us here today, not without jeopardizing what must transpire, so in the spirit of all things being equal we'll be bringing the festivities to them.

Full disclosure: this was always going to be a one-way trip, no matter how you received your ticket or the accommodations some of you might still believe are pending. I'll admit I was a bit on the nose with the name as well. *The You Deserve It Foundation?* I mean, come on. But it happened, you're here, and in time the P.O. boxes and answering machines will be linked back to me. Not all of you fell for it, of course, but when the majority of you did bite—this is what impressed me most. Your screaming and pleading though: music to my ears. Might be cliché, sure, but in a roundabout way it brings us back to who we're about to "drop" in on.

I found them in the pool house, my brother into a place my penis had never been, a place my wife assured me she would never, ever tolerate. What did I do when this occurred? I lost my mind. What else? But I continued to function as I have had to my entire life. Do you know why? Of course you do. Each of you preparing me in ways I would wish upon no one. It also meant I learned to adjust, to watch and wait and plan.

Means our descent began with a target in mind; a pool which took ten years of my life to pay off. And hey, would you look at that. Someone's home.

TOAD BASEBALL

I was eleven when I accidently killed my younger brother.

This is not the type of thing one hopes for while growing up, but there it is all the same, the power of it draining, drawn from me like a knife that eats at memory, the boy who was my twin.

I would say it defined me as well. How could it not?

Born John and Jason, we came into the world six minutes apart on the working side of West Virginia—two brothers, the McBlains, wailing at the world from the onset; two brothers awake and there to stay. This is what I tell myself whenever I think of the time we had together, there before it began—before I realized just how small we really, truly are.

Both of our parents were hard working and both of them held jobs. Mom ironed all day for the upper class, the dividing line of our town being Brock, which ran all the way down to Carrington. Dad was factory, pressing pipe until the fumes ate what lungs the place had left him to live his days with. We never wanted is what I'm saying. That is not to say that we were rich, not in the monetary way. They loved us is all, and both of us loved them—until what happened happened, of course.

It wasn't like I could blame them either. Hell, *I* hated me! Wanted nothing more than the power to wring my own neck as punishment for what I'd done. It didn't happen, of course, but boy had I wanted it. Years later, I continued to want it, but not as much as that first year; in time learning how to contain the self-hatred that seethed within me, allowing it to simmer and no more than for the waking hours of my day.

Night was a different beast altogether, chock full of all the ingredients every nightmare needs. They lessened as the years wore on, but they never went away, not fully. Sometimes I am in these dreams and sometimes I'm on the outside looking in, as if in third person. Jason is always there, every time, and so is the blood I took from him. He never speaks to me, not with his mouth. He usually just stands there on the patio and stares as the blood from the wound (a wound which, in the dream, has always been more exaggerated than it was in real life) at the side of his head slowly slides toward the ground where it will clump and collect like red cottage cheese. His eyes are empty in this dream, big white Os that look right through me. Occasionally he will lift his arm and point on toward something I never see. They are odd, these dreams, and I would be a liar if I said they no longer affect me.

So yes, I would say ending my brother's life holds a part in defining me. Hell, you could even argue it created someone altogether new. And for the record, I did not mean to, not ever, but it still does not change the fact that my hands were the ones swinging the bat that day.

Our backyard was small. Tiny, really, and almost identical to every other in the row of townhouses in which we lived. On either side of the sliding patio doors were window wells, each about three feet deep. They held stones, gravel, and the like at the bottom, forming a kind of bed. These window wells would sometimes hold toads as well, the creatures getting in there and nestling for warmth between what rocks they could negotiate. It is because of these toads that Jason and I were outside of our backyard that day—a place we both knew we should never go, not without some sort of protection. Be it Father, Mother, or tactical nuke.

His name was Rodney Bowers. He was the block bully and, man, did he live up to his name. A terror, really, and large for his age, which seems to be the way it goes, no? With bullies I mean, that they always seem big for their age; perhaps that's why they become bullies in the first place—too much mass and not enough brains to fill in the requisite space. To go with his size Rodney had a shovel for a face, wide, with his chin ending in some-what of a point. Small beady eyes overlooked a flat nose covered in freckles. He wore overalls too, if that helps set the scene.

And we knew to steer clear; all of us knew that Rodney and his band of terrors ruled the roost and woe the child crossing him and his boys coming to or from school, or just around the block. His cohorts smaller than him, but no less mean—sometimes meaner if given the chance. They were the Brady boys, Randy and Jeff, each brother not much more than a puddle in T-shirts and jeans. A year apart, they shared the same sense of god-awful humor—the type which seemed to laugh at a joke far too hard for far too long. They were nowhere near as funny as they thought they were either. But underneath that laughter laid meanness, as I have already mentioned. It was bone-deep in those two, double sharp and quick to cut. I have often believed that as Rodney became entwined with these two he was nothing more than accelerant to an already burning flame. Time would tell, and did. But that was after, near the end of their lives.

It is before I would like to discuss. Rodney, Randy, and Jeff were such tyrants that lunch money would be given over without even being asked for; that kids would push over one another to get out the door once the bell rang just to sprint their entire way home. They wanted no piece of what Rodney brought, no taste of what his kingship decreed. And who could blame them? We were smaller, weaker, each of us struggling to survive not only the current day at hand but what we knew to be coming: high school. Where bullies like Rodney became a dime a dozen, each a leader to the pack they chose. It would only get worse for kids like Jason and me. The way the world worked and had worked since time out of mind. Welcome to wonderland, people! Hang on to your hats and leave your money at the door!

He'd made a kid eat his own feces once—this being the story that stuck, the one which made the legend. After this the block became Rodney's, and more or less the school. Adam Clarke, who became Shit-Breath after the fact, had been the unfortunate soul in the washroom that day. In the first floor lavatory this was, between the fourth graders and the fifth. You would think something like this couldn't happen, not in elementary school, a civilized place of four hundred kids. Not too big a number nor too small. You would think a boy who had to move his bowels would be able to do so without fear of having to chew it up and re-swallow it down in front of a captive, laughing, guffawing audience of three. You would, wouldn't you? Not where Jason and I grew up. Not even close.

Poor kid had braces, too—the large kind, solar system and all.

Which more or less brings me back to the toads and the day we found them; back to the day when my brother's heart came shining through.

He always liked animals, always, ever since we were small. Dogs, cats, birds, what have you. It didn't matter. Be it insects or fish, spiders or frogs. He loved them *all*, always giving whatever creature catching his attention the best of what he was.

"How do you think they got in there?" This is what Jason asked me once we discovered the toads in the window well that day. I had no concrete answer for him—the well appearing much too high for a toad to climb. I suggested they burrowed their way in from somewhere we couldn't see. This seemed to appease him. It did not deter him from his objective of freeing them, however, which had become the goal the moment he noticed them.

"What if they starve," was his argument. I could not disagree with him. Nine toads later, all of them secured in Mother's Tupperware, our quest began.

I must stop here, but only for a moment. I wish to stress how much my brother loved animals. I know I have already mentioned this, but I don't know if I have explained it as fully as I could have. We had a dog once, a puppy. It developed cancer. Jason slept with that dog for three months straight while it succumbed. My parents finally had to take it away from him as the disease brought the dog close to the end. Jason would have none of it. He kicked and screamed, he cried and raged. It was his dog, *his,* and he was the one meant to help it home. I didn't understand what he was saying at the time, not then. But I came to years later, realizing just how mature my brother had been for his age. I think he thought he could heal, or that he was meant to be a protector of some kind. I'll never know, not for sure, but it's what I try to tell myself whenever the blackouts return.

Toads in Tupperware, we ventured out from the backyard, toward Rodney and his pals, though we didn't yet know it. We should have though, seeing as we had been living in fear of them for the better part of three years.

"Well whadda-ya-know! It's the freakin' Bobbsey twins!" Rodney exclaimed, his bushy brows gathering into the usual position. The one that says it is time to play, fuck you or otherwise. Immediate laughter followed this—the braying kind, from both Randy and Jeff. What came next was Rodney noticing what Jason held within his hands.

"What-choo got there, retard?" Rodney Bowers, ladies and gentlemen—the apex of our race.

"Toads," Jason said, no more. And to tell you the truth, I was surprised he had said anything at all. If there was one difference between my brother and me, I was the braver one. I do not say this to gloat. I say it simply as fact. I also do not say this to suggest I wasn't scared of Rodney—quite the opposite, matter of fact. It's that I have a line, and afraid or not, pushed hard enough, I will push on back. Fight or flight I believe it's called. Still, I should have realized.

"I can see that, numb-nuts. *What? You don't think I can see!?*" And there it was—what all bullies live and breathe on. They make it about themselves, projecting whatever junk they have on the inside onto whatever is readily available. They are self loathers, each and every one.

"No, that's not what I said." Besides what his words represented, I think it was a combination of them and what Rodney's eyes did—how they widened in disbelief—that caused my jaw to hit the ground. To be honest, it was amazing. My brother never showing me what he showed me that Saturday afternoon, never once in his too short life. Randy and Jeff stood exactly the same, their mouths replicas of mine, and perhaps time stood still there for a second or two, or perhaps it did not. Either way, the moment broke, replaced by an anger we knew all too well.

"Alright, fuck-o, you want to play, we can play!" Randy and Jeff came forward at that, as if soldiers at attention, but soldiers with greasy hair and unbrushed teeth. They had ball gloves as well, hanging from their hips, and in Randy's hand was the bag which contained their bats and balls. I then realized how we'd run into them; that the ball diamond was on the other side of the road past the end of our parking lot. They had been on their way to play a game, the two of us landing right in their way. As ever, I was a second too slow in registering what Rodney was about to do, but I saw it all in slow motion once it began; saw him ask Randy for a bat; saw Randy give him one as Jeff snatched the Tupperware container from out of Jason's hands; watched Rodney state that it was time for he and his friends to play a little of what he liked to call toad-baseball; saw him take up a toad, a larger one, watched him loft it into the air; listened to him shout "Batters up!" as he began to swing, his body all torque, his body coming round. Connecting, time turned normal, or seemed to, and the guts of the toad struck my face, entered my mouth. I was dumb-founded, shocked, but it was nothing compared to seeing my brother go at Rodney the way that he did.

It was a sight to behold. And I mean that, truly. Primal will be the word I use, because that's what I feel I saw.

He went to town on Rodney, first hitting him in the nuts and then right to his face as the bigger boy went down. The reason it worked is because it was the last thing Rodney expected. Remember, we were shorter than him by a foot, each of us fifty pounds lighter. Not to mention the fact that he'd had the neighborhood by the balls for the better part of three years. I imagine it was new to him. What he was feeling, I mean—because that's what I saw in the widening of his eyes: fear; big and round, dilated and yellow.

If only Randy and Jeff hadn't been there that day, then everything would have turned out differently. They *were* there however; each of them equal in becoming Rodney's saving grace.

They pulled Jason off their leader, scratching and clawing like girls. The grabbed and hit, they kicked and spat. Not until Rodney himself stood back up did it all turn to shit. Up, he went at my brother, sneering, hitting him hard in the gut not once, but twice. It was as he punched Jason in the face that I exploded; when I unleashed an amount of anger I have yet to feel again.

We were not angry children, neither of us. I want you to know this. It was the situation is all, and more than likely the entire three years prior; the whole time we had been subjected to the evil that was Rodney Bowers coming to a head right there on the dried out grass not thirty feet from the backyard we never should have left.

Bending down, I picked up the bat.

Going forward, I increased my pace.

Screaming, I swung.

Whenever I look back on that moment many things go through my mind. Not only *what* happened, but how

I see it happen; how it seems I now see it as I sometimes see myself in dreams, from that third person point of view. Years are the answer for this, I suppose; how time can be known to wear down a memory if it so chooses, fading it into a former version of itself. True or not, it is as clear as my picture comes when I think of that day.

I am swinging full bore. Not for Rodney's head, but for his shoulder. He is hurting my brother. I only want him to stop. I swing and I swing and again it all seems to slow down on me; the swing I have begun the only one I ever take. I continue to swing, to swing that same swing, and then slowly I begin to see Rodney move, to pull back and evade. Doing so, the bat misses him, but continues on the arc I have placed it on. I continue to swing, momentum imprisoning me. Too late, I realize I am powerless to stop what is about to occur.

The doctors tell us it was a perfect strike, or as close to a combination of a perfect strike as one could come; that the way Jason had been bent down, his head just past Rodney's hip—that the arc of the bat and the angle of his head…

Flush, the bat splits him open at the right temple. Brick-like, he crumbles to the ground like a building coming down.

I don't remember much after that. Not where Randy and Jeff and Rodney ran off to. Not how much time elapsed before our parents found us in the grass, one of their sons cradling the other in such a way as to make their mother scream until her voice runs dry. I don't remember any of those things, not one. What I do recall is feeling Jason die. Down the middle of my head, as the bat collided, I remember a snap, a crack—a *split* inside my mind. I don't have the words to fully describe what this was. It was there though, like a line of white pain running from the back of my head to the front. First time I felt anything like that, ever. With some twins it is said they can read each other's thoughts, know what the other is thinking—that they are that entwined. Jason and I didn't run like this, not once. What happened when he died was new. This is also what the doctors believed to be the cause of my blackouts.

They don't happen so much anymore, not like they did during that first couple of years after Jason died. One moment I would be watching *Little House on the Prairie* and the next I would find myself sitting outside the arcade down beside the plaza. People saw me. Even said I spoke with them when my parents really began to dig at why this was happening to me. Both the psychologist and psychiatrist they sent me to eventually told them—in better terms than this—to let it ride; that it was more than possible that this was just my way of dealing with the guilt. Made sense to me; made sense to them. We still moved however, despite the blackouts decreasing in frequency.

Littleton is where we ended up, the big city just north of New Dumfries and the life my parents wished to leave behind. Things improved with time, as things often have a habit of doing. Time heals all wounds, right? This is what they say. I can't say I totally buy into such a thing, but I will say it is something to consider when the bleakness sets in and all seems lost. My blackouts? Regrettably, they remained a part of my life for quite some time, but continued to lessen the older I became. Between episodes, three years was the longest I went without losing time. This was during my sophomore year. Unfortunately, this was also the time the murders began.

Was it me? The unknown person of interest they labeled the Campus Killer? I don't know and can't say with any degree of certainty. It was Rodney Bowers who had caused my—then—latest blackout; that me running into him on campus nine years removed from the day with the toads sparked what I think I have secretly feared since the moment Jason died.

Walking home from chem-lab was when it happened, and he noticed me before I could notice him. He had a beard now, close cut and red. His face was no longer a child's, not puffy nor chunky nor young. Nevertheless, it held the shape I remembered it having. Not as pointy at the chin, but still as overly wide. His eyes remained exactly the same however, small and hateful—a thing I have never forgotten. Eyes like that never change, not once they've matched the heart within.

"Well, if it isn't one half of the Smothers brothers! What's up, baby killer? How you been?" It must have been my face, what he registered on it. From the moment he said it, you could see he wished he could retract the words. After that I can tell you nothing. Not for an entire two week period. Oh, I have speculations, don't you worry—as well as assumptions. I can prove nothing, of course, not without admitting to something I am not even sure I have been a part of.

He'd been murdered, you see. Rodney. He and three others, all women, during a span of time I have yet to regain. The position this put me in...I would wish it on no one. Not only because of the history Rodney and I shared, but because of his cause of death: blunt force trauma to the base of the neck. Some type of heavy instrument bashing in the back of his skull.

It had echoes, you see—shades of a bloody, if not symmetrical past.

I was never questioned, not once, and the killings ended as abruptly as they began—what the papers printed repeatedly as the months wore on. Was it another coincidence? Blind luck that Rodney had chosen to enroll in the very same university as the kid whose brother he helped to inadvertently kill? In another city fifty miles removed from where no one knew of the connection which bound us? Perhaps, but no, I do not believe it. Not so much and not anymore. The reason for this was because of what I found in my basement not a month ago. I share this house with my wife and our twin two-year-old girls. New Dumfries is the town we now live in, the same New Dumfries my parents moved me from all those years ago. We have been here four years now, the clinic I opened the reason and choice.

What I found was a collection of ball bats in a bag behind the furnace. They were not new, these bats. They were old, used. They were stained as well, with little chunks of God knows what sticking to the ends.

This was not my bag; one I do not remember purchasing. This means next to nothing of course, as I have lost more time than I care to remember (or *not* remember, because really, how would I know?) as the days of my life progressed. Not large amounts in the scheme of things, no, but enough if I am to be honest, the incidents growing with some regularity at about the time we moved back here. This is what scares me now, when I look back over my life, especially since Jason's death. I think of that *split* a lot, that feeling I had the moment he died. It led me places I never thought I would go; the library, for one, and its research rooms for another. I wanted answers, you see, definitive and concrete. Did I get them? Depends on how you look at it.

Broken down, Twin to Twin Transfusion Syndrome is when one twin steals from another without knowing they are doing so. Blood for instance, where one twin, usually the bigger of the two, hoards much of the supply, thereby ensuring his identical brother or sister is born smaller. Intriguing, no? Perhaps when I finish putting it in perspective, then.

I was the bigger twin; what my mother always told us. Keeping in mind TTTS, what if such a thing could continue outside the womb? Insane, right? Of course it is. Does that make it any less plausible?

What if at the moment of Jason's death—what if I did the very same thing I did when we were still inside our mother? And what if instead of absorbing his blood, I took on his soul? It would explain some things. Like how I can miss weeks at a time but everyone I come in contact with during that time admits to noticing nothing out of the ordinary about me. How can that be? Unless someone more than a little like me…someone who might be *identical* to me in almost every conceivable way…

Also, remember how I told you that Jason liked animals—that he *loved* them?

I graduated a veterinarian for God's sake! A *vet*! Does one need any more proof? Okay. Last bit of information and then I will go. And this is the part which has been keeping me up at night; the stuff that turns my stomach so cold I can sometimes taste it at the back of my throat. The baseball bats, of course—the means by which Jason died. Can you imagine the anger one would have as that happened? The rage it would create the instant before you died? I know I can, being as I was the one who was there. But it's the tapes which are freaking me out! There are two of them now, both of them in the bag of bats and both of them marked WATCH ME. I did not put them there, and only one had been in there when I first found the bag. I know who it is. Deep down, I really do. But do I want to talk to him? That is the question, and the one which begs it all. In the end, who am I really: the shadow of a boy long past gone or, quite simply, my own fractured self?

Does it make sense to you, how my life appears? Would you tell me if it did? Seriously, I am running out of options here. I mean, when I start to think I feel him moving around up there, what's a man to do? Seriously, what does something like this say about a person? What can it?

I love my daughters and my wife. If anything, I will always have that.

SIZE MATTERS

Go big or go home. This is what I remember most about my father. He was other things as well, but that motto is what sums him up most whenever he enters my mind.

"Jimmy? What the fuck?" Nicky said.

From the couch I respond—holding up a hand now a couple digits shy of what used to be the norm.

Nicky's face contorts in an instant, the concern I'd seen as he came through the door gone and replaced by a rage that matched my own. It was Dad-rage, round and bold, minus any type of middle ground. Go big or go home indeed.

"Bastard said it was you, Nicky. What I owed for the guns fuck-up. Said I should be grateful you were letting me live at all."

Nicky stood there breathing hard, clenching and unclenching his fists. His father's son alright. A sight Nicky and I had been privy to many times growing up, receiving end or otherwise.

"And Lime was there?"

"Big man did the deed himself. Couple of prospects holding me down as he did." Buck Lime was the man in question, Nicky's second in command. *You really sure about this, Jimmy? I mean, Nicky's the only family you got left.*

I was sure then and I am more than sure now.

I take a drag of my smoke and then chug the rest of my beer. The hand hurts doing this, but the loss of bone would be worth the price of admission once things played themselves out. If Nicky was the reflection of our father then I was the personification of our mother: methodical, patient, and aware of all the angles presented in any given situation. It's how I got to where I now stood—number three in terms of position in spite of my age. Only reason I wasn't one better was because of the very same thing, and that Nicky and Lime had come up together, thick as goddamn thieves, each of them present when Dad first formed the Club. I was about to usurp this—to show that cooler heads would always prevail.

"I didn't sanction this, Jimmy. I want you to know that." I was counting on Nicky going there. Angles, you see. Angles. Angles. Angles.

"Your call, bro," I say and hold my hands up and out, little runs of blood still seeping from my bandaged left hand. Nothing more needed to be said, not then. Nicky's anger would take care of the rest. It would get me to where I wanted to be. A sit-down called by Nicky himself.

The deal was mine and mine alone. Ever since I found out it was them and not McNauly who'd taken out Dad. For months I'd been working on Buck, planting the idea of running the show inside his meathead brain. It didn't take much. Not at first and certainly not now. Nicky on the other hand—I would need to give something up in order for what I wanted to come to pass. The last two fingers of my left hand seemed as good a tool as any.

Bold moves. Big things. This is what it takes to lead, Jimmy.

I believed him. We both did. Thing was Nicky took his belief a little too far. Chose to believe his little brother incapable of the rage he lived with on a daily basis as well. He was wrong. So very fucking wrong. And for it he was about to be sent home. Him and Lime both.

Going big now, Dad. Get ready for some guests.

IN PREPARATION

Could it be covered up?

This is the question I asked myself as I stood over her lifeless body, my chest a heaving mess, her face the very same. I have done many things in the fifty-six years I have been alive. Things I am proud and ashamed of, and things I'm sure I can no longer recall. I have loved and lost, I have cried and laughed. There has been heartache and pain coupled with the death of a child and a disdain for the world we're born to occupy. Happiness has been there too though, and joy, along with the security which comes from the middle holding strong. I have had an average life is what I'm getting to, no greater or worse than any other once you divide it down.

For twenty-five years I have held the same job and for five more I'd been married to the same woman who up until yesterday continued to share my bed. Her name was Martha—she who was my rock.

It was she who turned me; Martha who succeeded for more than twenty years at keeping the beast within me at bay. I was a serial killer, you see, or am, depending on how you choose to look at it. In all the years we shared a life she never knew of my extra-curricular activities. I want that to be known. And I want this on the record, the one I'm sure too soon will come. How could she not know? No doubt some will say this once everything is said and done, and precisely because of that is why I am writing this—what any would call their last confession.

I have always been a narcissist, but a selective one at that. I feel I am above the self-admiration associated with such people. I *am* self-centered though, and of that you may be sure. I will not shy away from this part of my disorder, nor have I ever. It is who I am, nature undenied.

Like any good sociopath I have many tics and behaviors. Throughout the years I have learned to suppress many of these while mimicking others; what society has deemed the norm. This was not easy, not at first, but in time I managed to stick and hold the landing. My lack of empathy was hardest for me fake, that and remorse, which up until sometime yesterday I'm pretty sure I'd yet to feel. Martha was the one who saved me—which I think I've already alluded to—Martha who helped me find the middle I've as well already mentioned; her face, her beauty; her kind, kind soul. She was one in a million, my Martha, a woman so selfless I am still having a hard time believing she is gone.

In 1981 she was to be my sixth victim. Instead she became my wife—a woman who bore me a child and then helped me bury that same child eighteen years later. I have never recovered from Donavan's death. I admit this freely and without shame while acknowledging that his death was most likely the tipping point which brought the killer inside me back out to play. It was the hollowness I felt inside, you see, this slick feeling which seemed to coat the lining of my stomach. It angered me, threatening my way of life. Did I say anger? I meant fury. *Livid.* And beyond unfair that he had been ripped from us—that we had taken the time to raise and nurture him, teach and believe in him, and then when his life was at the ripening point...his wings...spread...that cancer would intercede and cut him down to a shell of what he'd been. I'd have killed him myself if I thought I could have gotten away with it. Looking back, I believe right then is when the monster inside me awoke. And no, the irony is not lost on me—I'd now had someone ripped from me just as I had ripped from the lives of countless others. I do not deny this, nor do I embrace it. It is only the narcissist in me, a trait I think I've explained.

"Can I help you?" Those four words were the first she had ever spoken to me. She had strawberry-blonde hair back then, cut in a bob, and a series of freckles which rested across the bridge of her nose. With light-green eyes and lips I wanted to slit, she was bending down to pick up the oranges I dropped on my way out the door.

I had been in the grocer not for groceries that day but because of her; weeks earlier, as I was making my way home, she had found my eye. I followed her, discovered first where she worked and then that her name was Martha. I thought she was to be my next victim, one who like the others would scream as I ripped the flesh from her face and then her face from her skull. This changed however—changed instantly—in the moment she looked into my eyes while passing me the oranges I'd fumbled near the door. There was something between us then, a spark, different from anything I had felt before. Her touch, as she placed her hand over mine, was soft, gentle, honest, arousing in me something beyond the sexual, outside the primal. I was fascinated, spinning. The woman whom I had wanted to maim and rape and kill had somehow affected me on a level I was unaware I possessed. Had she broken through with just a touch? Was this all it took, really? I didn't know; not then, nor now. But both are things I have thought long and hard about as the years wore on, challenging myself to find an answer which would somewhat satisfy. I am sorry to say I still have found nothing save Martha herself; her being and her grace.

She tamed me, really. For lack of a better word, she neutered a stone-cold killer with a bat of her eye, the touch of her skin. The sociopath smitten, my desire to sever her neck from her shoulders became a thing of the past, dissolving, replaced by a need to know everything about her—but by choice, hers, not force, mine. This was the key—that she could stir in me something other than the tendencies which had ruled me since before the summer of '74.

It was all I could do not to fumble for words. Oranges up, I asked her out. With a smile she agreed and the rest, as they say, is history. A good history, if I do say so myself. We had our ups and downs, yes, all married couples do, but for the most part it was a happy time, a time where I actually *felt* and was no longer pretending as I once had—my mask in place for the world to see. It was genuine what I was feeling, you see, which I'm sure is the reason why my need to kill went dark. It had been replaced by the love of a woman who stood outside the sum of her parts—a wife who was true to her man, her life and her marriage, and was of the type who put her needs behind all others, her husband's especially.

And I know you are thinking sexual and for the most part you'd be right, though this was not always the case, as the emotional aspect of our lives had its quirks and spurts as well. Where Martha was open and engaging all the time, I seldom was. She worked at me however, worked hard, and because of this I have over the years become quite the conversationalist—people no longer staring as they once did whenever I laughed at a joke being told during a party. She refined me is what I am saying, teaching me everything I should have been taught by parents who should have taken the time to love me.

But the sex! *My God!* The sex is what destroyed me. As free and giving as Martha was outside the bedroom, it was when we found ourselves within that she truly knew no bounds; her selflessness amplified. "Come," she would say, whispering into my ear. "I want you in my mouth." When she would say things like this...they filled me...that *she* wanted *me*...that I would never again have to take. This was part of it as well. How I think she put to sleep the more dangerous parts of what I was before we met. Her appetite for intercourse so large and so unabashed that it enveloped me, quashing any thoughts or needs I might find in the arms of murder. Martha did this unintentionally though, and I want that to remain clear—she had no idea as to what she was bottling as she soothed and sucked and fucked. She was only pleasing the man she knew of then, not the man I'd been before.

Insatiable, I tried to please her but could never keep up. It wasn't so much that I *couldn't*, but Martha, as I said—she only wished to please. I mean, there would be days when my penis fought to leave her mouth. *Days!* That is how selfless she was, how much she lived to please. I miss her. Really, I do.

Those days are over though. Long gone and dead, like the boy. Had the cancer not taken him, he would've been twenty-eight this fall, a man in his own right. He was smart too, smarter than us both. He had his mother's eyes and the line of my jaw. He never should have died, my son. Actually, he never should have been born, but God's humor, it ain't so much in the department of ha-ha if you know what I mean; that Donavan, by dying, became the catalyst which set the killer in me free. His death awakening in me once more the need to render and violate; to *balance* the violation someone had seen fit to throw our way. As I hurt, so would others. It was only fair. I thought this then. I do not think this now. I have changed. Martha's death has seen to that.

So twenty years after a woman's love restrained a beast the beast was back and open for business. And as they say—it *was* like coming home.

I started small, baby steps, wading into the shallow end of the pool—the woman was in her twenties, pretty, and bound and gagged before she knew what hit her.

She screamed as I remembered them screaming and died the very same. The very last light of life winking out of her eyes as I looked down on her from above, her head held softly in my the palm of my hand. Door to door I continued on, selling insurance to those who would least suspect. An acceptable cover, selling insurance—always had been—then as well as later, after what happened with the boy. Made it easier to scout out and take notes of who lived alone and who did not. For five years this continued, five years after the death of our son. It was then I got sloppy.

It's frustrating, you know—this part of it. I mean, it's not like I don't know, but more to the effect that I have a hard time understanding the meaning behind the why of *why* we embrace it. I mean, seriously, you would have to be out of your fucking mind to attempt such a thing— and hey, yes, I will call a spade a spade, but truly, *all of us*? Down to the most inept of us? It has to be the narcissism, has to. There is no other way around it. I mean, why else would men like me feel the need to keep some sort of article which relates to their victims? It's idiotic! No, reckless, foolish. Lacking the minimum amount of common sense the worst of us should have. Is it because deep down we *want* to get caught? Is this why our judgement is so off? It doesn't make sense. No, not now that I see it in hindsight. Why would we keep these trinkets in the first place? Is it inherent, brought on by the conceit of us? It would appear so, as history shows— the ones you read about doing it again and again. Some guy collecting ears he kept in a jar to another who would take only jewelry to which he and only he could masturbate to at half past the crazy hour. Doesn't matter. Not what it *is*, but that we *do* it. Some little part of us. It wants to get caught, must. This is all I can figure. Why else had I kept their licenses?

Yep, licenses. That was my thing. Sometimes health cards and the like but only when this was all they had. The cards were bound by elastic and sealed within a Ziploc bag I held in a box in my shed below the second to last floorboard beneath my workbench. Do I have to explain how unwise something like this can be? Sure I had my safeguards, who wouldn't? But did I honestly think it would ever happen? No, I did not. It did however, and only because of a portrait painted by my son.

Hanging in the main hall leading into our living room, Donavan had created the picture in sixth grade in honor of Martha's thirty-first birthday. Years later, unbeknownst to any of us, it would become the linchpin which outed me. The string attached to either side of the portrait, the one which hung upon the nail coming out from the wall, this is what broke. And this is what sent Martha out to the shed that night. Did the nail she went to get fall from her hand? Is this what happened? Did it roll? I don't know. Still, I have a hard time understanding why she would be in the shed looking for nails when all she needed was a new length of string from the drawer in the kitchen. No matter. What's done is done and what's found was found. What upsets me is how it affected her. I pictured her finding the licenses and at first denying it once she realized what they could signify.

After that, knowing Martha, she would try to rationalize what she was dealing with. It wouldn't happen. No, not if I knew Martha. Which I do...did. Later, I would find the trail she left on her laptop. The one which had linked some of my trips to some of the towns and cities the licenses said the woman were from. Quite the investigator my little Martha had become, doing all this in between the time I called to check in—which I always did whenever I was on the road for more than two days at a time—to the time I returned. It was then, as I spoke with Martha over the phone, that I knew something was off. It was minute but *there,* her octave just shy. These are the things you know after thirty years of marriage, things that only one other could ever come to know.

Anyway, I knew she knew but did not let her know I suspected. I couldn't, not then, when the phone I was on was the only device I had at my disposal. I drove home instead, speeding six hours straight. During this time was when I decided not to kill her, certain that reason and the assurances I would give would be enough to see me through. I would tell her I had stopped once before and that the reason for this had been her. This worked in my head better than it did in real life, as she agreed with me in every scenario I could conjure, especially the one where she fully understood and realized that the death of our son had shaken me so much that I could not be blamed for lashing out at the world as I did. That it, not me, was at fault because of what it had done to me. She would even go so far in saying it was on par to what my father had put me through growing up on the farm.

Fantasies, all of it—the mind of a madman—except for the truth which of course came next.

As I rounded the corner which led to our street, I knew I was taking a chance that Martha had instead called the police once she found my souvenirs and I was moments away from driving myself right into the walls of a cell which would before too long end with me strapped to a chair. Either way, I was beginning to have the feeling that I had become more than fucked from Sunday.

Headlights off, I continued forward, around the bend. All was quiet. All was dark—save for our bedroom where the light was still on. Inside, I checked her computer and found exactly what I thought I might. Martha had been busy since last we spoke. Next I went out back and checked the floorboard in my shed, the one which held my secret. Sure enough, the fine dust of shavings had been disturbed. Pulling out the box, I examined the cards. Close, but the order was incorrect. Allison Jersey was *before* Brenda McClellan, not after. Martha had tried, yes, but failed. It was time to talk.

Onwards I went, upstairs, toward the bedroom and Martha's sleeping frame. On her side as always I watched her steadied breaths, looked on and reminisced. How would I begin? What would be the magic words? From the beginning, then—this is what I thought as I spoke her name to wake her. Instead she attacked me; verbally, not physically, though it might as well have been. If I didn't know it before, I sure as hell knew then: my wife's compassion—it was not a thing to be trifled with. Martha had always been a strong and upfront person, this you know. What I might have failed to interpret was how deep and far that compassion for any one person could go. Me I've explained. How she suppressed in me this need to kill, if only for a while. She approached this in many ways: physically, emotionally and intellectually. But not just for me. For *everyone* she met in life, be it family, friend, or foe. It was elegant; *she* was elegant, the way she conducted herself. What I am trying to say is that I was caught off guard as I stood beside our bed and she roared up out of it, her rage at the ready, full and dark and much like venom. Shocked, I stepped back, trying to gain my bearings. It was extraordinary what I was witnessing, unprecedented, from a woman who in the previous thirty years had not so much as furrowed a brow at me. A *brow!* She had raised her voice, sure, who hasn't? But the display I was beholding, the ferocity of it...

"Seriously, you are my *husband!*" she said, her voice all fury, her face much the same. "How is it that you are even capable of this? You're nothing! *We're* nothing! The meek—isn't that what you said? That we'd inherit the earth? Murray, you're a goddamn insurance salesman for Christ's sake! How can something like this be inside you?" Those words haunt me still, the last she ever spoke. And do you know why? Would you like to? I thought you might. You've come this far, why not a little further? It was the look, you see, the one which danced upon the steel now set in the green of her eyes. I knew it, and I knew it well. It was the look every woman I have ever taken saw in *my* eyes before they died by my hand.

If I did not end Martha then she was very much about to kill me. This is what I want you to know; this is what I wish to confess.

Which brings me back to the question I began with: *Could it be covered up?*

However, before I go on with that, I want to get something off my chest. Something I realized not long ago. It has to do with my unchecked narcissism. I say unchecked now because I was wrong before, earlier when I said I did not need the admiration associated with my condition. I am a big enough man to admit this. Why else would I have told Martha how I liked to do them? Why else would I leave a signature every single time? Yeah, it's about me. All of it. Always has been, always will be. Did you know they even have a name for me? Did I mention that? "The Wrecker" is what the papers say—what I've been *deemed*. It's because I destroy their faces, you see. Not only, but mostly. The other reason is because I remove the jaw—the bottom half, taking most of the neck as I rip down to pull it free.

So...could it be covered up; this is what I'd been thinking at the beginning as I began to write this. Is that really the kind of question a story should start with? And believe me, this *is* a work of fiction: nothing in the above sentences actually happening. Did you see that coming? Well, did you? You're probably thinking I'm fucking with you now, yes? Or someone is anyway. *What is happening?* could this be what's running through your head? Or perhaps: *Where is the author*

Beau Johnson

going with this? Better yet: *Have I missed a page, possibly some crucial point of plot?* They're all good questions, every one. But the truth? The truth is now— me and you; what I do. My MO is simple. I watch. I wait. I see. I scout. Gathering information, I see if the person I have chosen lives alone or not. Satisfied, I continue to wait, continue to watch. I look for boyfriends. I look for girlfriends. I watch for parents who visit much too often and stay far too late. After this is when I take it to the next level; when I write a story similar to the one you hold in your hands. I then address it to you, my intended victim, and leave it between your doors. But that's where I found *this* is what you might be thinking now. This is when the fear should set in, when you're almost in the know. I then go back to waiting, observing from somewhere close. I have installed cameras in your house, the type you've failed to see. You will look around as you are doing now but still you will not see; they are tiny, these devices, and very state of the art. Once I know you are reading and once I know you're near the end I slip in undetected and travel up your stairs. Sometimes they creak as I climb and sometimes they don't. I walk soft; I do, but sometimes still I'm heard. Is that me now is what I'm saying, out beyond your door? My feet now off the rise and stepping ever close?

To those who know me, I am a nondescript white male who blends well within a crowd. For those who don't, I have taken over two dozen people in my lifetime.

To you I say prepare.

163

A BETTER KIND OF HATE

First time I meet Lamar Purdue is in another life.

Squat for his age, he's thicker at fourteen than the height he'd come to be in all his years.

Little man had a hound dog face and jerry curl eyes. He was polite too, politer than most, which is why things played out the way they did I suppose. All his *Yes, sirs* and *No, sirs* music to my rookie ears. The coldness in his eyes I didn't see until later, at his hearing, and then behind bars. Rookie mistake number one. You cannot fix things. You can only try. Not me, though. Not then. I knew things. I was there to save the day.

I didn't know a damn thing.

We found Lamar's mom slumped in a chair, the back of her head now the top of her throat.

"Lamar. I'm Detective Rider. This is Detective Batista. You up for some questions?" I look over at Batista and he gives me the nod. *Go ahead, kid, it's your show.* We'd been partners three weeks. Three weeks and this was the first time he'd given me the reins.

"She said her banana...said it tasted like suicide." Poor kid is what we thought, but that was it, the kid and our investigation giving us nothing more than what it looked like. Three months later I enter another house to find Lamar. He's on the steps, same hound-dog face, same jet-black eyes. His hands are bound behind his back though, cuffed and ready to go. Doesn't take me much to figure it out from there.

The foster family he'd been living with had been gutted and then cut into more manageable pieces. By the look of the tub and the bottles of bleach beside, Lamar was looking to try something new.

"Don't let it wear on you too much, kid. Sociopaths will always be the hardest ones to catch." Batista was right, but even then, it still didn't sit.

Kuwait had yet to start.

April and my mother were still alive.

But I could not save lives because I had yet to fully see.

I see now, though. I see very well indeed. So does Lamar, even after I go to town on his eyes.

"That all you got, Rider?" He'd been released this morning, seventeen years to the day we shut him down. From behind I stayed close, followed him to an IHOP just off the 15, picked him up just as he sat to eat. "'Cause they're worse than you from where I been." I move forward, toward the chair, and put a bullet through his right knee.

He screams. Curses. Other knee bouncing up and down like mad.

"Man, you was a cop once! This ain't right!"

"And all you've done is?" He stops at that, and then everything is still. We look at each other. I see the future as well as the past. I want to go back. I want to see the murder hidden in that young punk's eyes. I want to stop what he did. I can't though, and I know that, just as I know I will never stop what I do; what men like Lamar have forced me to become. I'd like to say its centrifugal force, that something is pushing me on, that it's pulling as well, but it's not and I realize as much.

It's just a different kind of killing. A better kind of hate.

It's here I begin to cut.

KNIT ONE, PURL TWO

You will never change. I know that now. I mean, of all men, me and you combined, did you really not once envision this playing out as it has? Tough call, agreed, but the look on your face tells me more than you're willing to admit, I think. 'S'okay, though, we're almost to the end of it.

Twenty years is what I gave you, Frank. Twenty years without me saying a word. You'd think a thing like that could buy a bloke anything he desired. That silence for freedom could be a pact any sane man could abide. Couldn't be done though, could it, Frank? Whatever would a man of my skill set do with nothing but time on his hands? Isn't that what you said that very first day? It was in your Caddy, no? You and your driver idling right outside the gate? For truth, I think this might have been the exact moment I knew we'd end up coming to heads. Not twenty years ago, not when we were the same. And don't get me wrong, I understand how you see things. But I will not accept everything, Frank. Not after how much I have taken for the team. A man changes is what I have been trying to get through to you. Sometimes this is for good, Frank, sometimes for not so good. The man, he changes regardless. Doing so whether you approve of it or not. You would have none of it though, would you?

Nope. Not one goddamn ounce.

Which brings us to here, to today, with me awake and you in a chair. I say awake because you've done what you intended to do, Frank. You've ended up on the wrong side of the fence, sure, but when you go and poke the bear long enough this usually becomes the case. You were the first person I heard use this phrase, Frank. You know that? I say it to prove a point. Blink if I need to elaborate.

The portable wood-chipper stays in the past though, as I've said. It was the thing that got me put away—it will never become the thing which places me back. I think you fail to understand this part of it as well. That I would ever want to chance the *possibility* of going back! You had other plans, as men like you usually do. Angers me, all of it, but all it really does is bring me back to what you wanted.

And that you'll never change.

And let there be no doubt that this is because of you. My time spent inside changing the man I was into the man I've become. In six short weeks you have destroyed all of this, Frank. What do you suppose something like that deserves? What would the old me do? Better yet, what would the old you have the old me do if I were still in your employ? Again, the wood-chipper remains dead, and just between us, I never really thought the machine suited me, not as it should. Always liked to see the look on the faces last a little bit longer than the time it took to send a body through. Surprised? Good. I'd have it no other way.

I can tell you they teach trades on the inside. Crafts as well. You know what it is I learned inside, Frank? Learned to crochet is what I did. Knit one, purl two, and all that happy crappy. Brought peace of mind is what this did. Allowing me to grow as a human being and taking me away from all the shit I used to do.

Until now that is.

You understand what it is I'm saying here, Frank?

You understand why your children, your grandchild-dren, your girlfriend and wife are sitting here beside you? The tears are helping, as well I bet regret, but what it comes down to is what you wanted just not who you wanted it done to.

I'm going to open them up, Frank. Just so you know. Then I'm going to stitch together what comes out. Done, it's on to what I will refer to as patterns. What we in the crotchet business sometimes call blossoms. It will involve back posting, fastening off and an absolute favorite of mine, the invisible decrease. When it's complete, Frank, when it is, this is when I'm going to tell you the last thing you'll ever hear: you shouldn't have poked the bear, Frank.

Better yet, you should have accepted I'd changed.

WONDER TWIN
POWERS, ACTIVATE

The one in the Hulk mask says, "The way this works is we give you a head start. Makes it more equal than it'd be otherwise." I look at him through the bars of the cage, through the strings of dark hair that hang before my eyes. Of the three he was the bigger one, dressed in khakis and Nikes which looked impossibly small on a man so tall. His shoes were not what interested me though. What did is what he'd just explained. That things were about to begin. Allowed me to breathe deep for the first time in hours. For the first time in days, really. Done, I continued my part. Added a little quiver to my voice just to be sure. "Does that mean I get some clothes now?"

I don't receive a response, just a tilt of the Hulk's head.

Yeah, pretty sure I'd do him last.

Long story short is my sister'd gone missing. Before she does she's able to text me: *In trouble. Happened at the bar. Maddy's. Two guys I think. Maybe three! Done this before for sure! I'm sorry, Cass. Should have known.*

Shannon was not as stupid as she let on. A little too trusting perhaps, but that was just our mother making herself known. With me it was a different story. All Dad, all business, all the time. Made my life a bit more difficult than I wanted it at times but boo-fucking-hoo, we all have baggage. That right there makes me seem tougher than I actually am. Coping mechanism, maybe? In response to a life devoid of as many hugs as it should have had? I'll take who-gives-a-fuck for two hundred, Alex. Maybe throw in a chaser of lick-my-clit for good measure.

Leads me to do what any type of person like me would. I don't call the cops, don't pass go and collect two hundred dollars. Instead I haul ass to the little shit-burb Shannon ended up, Brantford, and set up shop in a Motel 6 the other side of what they call the Lorne Bridge. Hunk a junk is more like. Covered to the tits in graffiti done by someone wearing what I can only assume was a helmet. Next I'm at the bar, Maddy's, but I'm going about things slow, asking no questions, just observing. It's dark, a dive, and full of drowning lives from eleven a.m. until about nine. After that the younger crowd from the university slides in, and here is where I get my first nibble.

"I've seen you here before. Last week, right?" I do my best at being something I'm not.

"That's not going to get you very far if you're trying."

"Who said I was?" It did as intended, eliciting a smile I'm sure quite a few women had already seen. From the end of the bar I notice another man, shaggier than white teeth here, and suddenly it's on, as I feel I'm in their crosshairs. Which was fine, exactly what I wanted, and so I let white teeth go and purchase the remainder of the night's drinks. His bud, "Roger," comes over when we're on our fourth. I say hi to mustache-man, pat his mounded chest, and play the part Shannon has always played so well.

I should probably back up here and let you know Shannon had a problem. Many, if I'm to be honest. Meth was her bad boy though, the woman for years living on the chip. Some would say it was because our father was a cop and our mother a whore. I say Shannon just liked the easy things in life. I suggest it's why we're such opposites, and why Dad seemed to like me best. When I say things like this, I know it doesn't help the situation, not really, but it is what it is, and me being here now is perhaps my way of atoning. Who knows though, right? I mean, I *am* on my period.

Back to it, then.

Whatever they slip into my drink does the trick and the next thing I know I'm on my stomach, naked, and in a cage with one third of the Avengers staring me down.

"Hello, beautiful," They say, each of them in singsong unison. "Time to play."

Fuck they were going to burn.

I learned a lot of things in Afghanistan. Some I have implemented, some I have yet to. I'm about to explain the things I'd yet to. It involves cracks and crevices and devices small enough to slip within such places undetected. I inserted a cherry-colored butt-plug as well, just in case the decision to rape me in the ass came into question once they had me where they wanted me. Couldn't see them going to the extra trouble if I already had something blocking an entrance. Figured they go for the easiest route possible.

I needn't have worried.

I was naked, sure, but I had yet to be breached.

"Your dicks must be pretty damn small," I say and pull myself to my knees. I wanted to stand but the dimensions I'd awakened to would not allow me this wish. The middle one, Spidey, laughed hard at this. I mean really hard. Meant one of two things. I'm sure you can figure out which.

"We got a live one here, boys!" Iron Man says, and I throw it back just as fast as I can. They don't appreciate my candor, none of them, but only the Hulk steps forward in an attempt to kick what fingers I had wrapped around the bars.

"Hulk smash!" I say, and I'm not the only one who laughs.

The Hulk turns to Iron Man, "What the fuck, man?"

"What? It was funny." The Hulk doesn't move in response to this; just stands and stares at his buddy who is just about as tall as Robert Downey Jr., but you know, minus the lifts. "Let's just do this then. Wouldn't want anyone to make you angry." This gets Spidey going, and suddenly it's just a laugh riot between the two of them, each of them doubled over. It let me know the Hulk was not the alpha male of the group. It also meant things were looking up.

"You think we can do this?" Petulant. Hollow. Yep, third in line for sure.

"Go ahead," Iron Man says. And the Hulk does. I was to die, I'm told, but I would at least be given a fighting chance. Sporting of them, I said, but was instructed to shut the fuck up for my trouble. They had done this many times before, the Hulk goes on, with no one escaping ever. He repeats *ever* and I couldn't help but think how easy this was going to be once they let me out.

"And you can run as far and fast as you can. We don't care. We will find you. We will have you. Then we will kill you."

"This is your regular spiel?" I couldn't help myself. I tried. I really did. And if there is anything I would change about myself it would be this: sometimes I am just as arrogant as fuck.

It's more or less why I didn't see the cattle prod and then why I only saw dark.

And then we are back to where we began, and the Hulk turns from me, the quiver just gone from my voice. He turns back with my bra and the jeans one of them had gone and cut into short-shorts. He throws them at me, my nipples in awe. Cold, really, as the basement was as far from warm as it was from furnished. Drafty, the air came tinged with not only the smell of me but perhaps Shannon as well. Maybe at the start, sure, but I doubt as the days wore on.

Dressed, the Hulk does what the Hulk does best, and once again I'm "smashed." When I awake this time I am alone and the cage is open, the game afoot. Not a game, not really, but it might as well have been. Outside the cage I stand and hear my bones applaud. Done, I reach around and remove the butt plug. Deeper in and to the left is where I have stored a different kind of three inches. Extended it turns into nine, and the heft that comes is good.

I clean it off in the corner, in an old washtub. I relieve myself and drink greedily from the faucet as well. The lights flicker. Flicker again. The caged fluorescents in front of the washtub going out completely as the ones above me finish their dance. A familiar chuckle comes next, followed by all four as they come out from behind the stairs. Shannon leads the way. She is weaponless. The others are not. The Hulk carries his prod but Iron Man and Spidey now hold steel.

"I knew you'd come," Shannon says. Yes, she is high. She still looks good though, her color better than I imagined. "You've brought a knife to a gun fight though. You remember what Daddy use to say about that?" Have I mentioned my sister hates me? That she always has? I should probably explain the rest of it then, now that we've come to the end.

"You can't really believe I didn't know, can you? Shannon, you punctuated every sentence in the text you used to get me here. You think the fear you were trying to project, you think any rational person would afford themselves the time? It reinforces you as the stupid one." I get Iron Man with this one, a full blown pig snort from beneath his mask. As Spidey and the Hulk turn toward him it gives way to the type of opportunity that usually presents itself. Sometimes you have to nudge things along, sure, but most of the time it's just pieces falling into place.

To her credit Shannon sees it coming but her reflexes are nowhere near what a person needs them to be. Her eyes, however, are the opposite of this. Each of them becoming big white Os just about as fast as they can. She takes it under the chin, the blade up and through the soft palette of her mouth, the one which had probably been filled with something other than food as she went and sold me out. *I can get her here,* I hear her say, *someone better for you to hunt. She was in the war,* I hear her plead, but then I'm back and I remove the knife and Shannon just falls to the concrete floor with a thud.

We stand there, this new Fantastic Four, and all we do is breathe and regard each other for what feels like minutes. I decide to take it upon myself. "You guys want to do this proper then? Maybe side with a woman who can get shit done?" They continue to look at me and then at each other. It's Iron Man who laughs first, a sardonic little thing. Spidey joins and then so does the Hulk. I take it as a sign. I have landed on my feet once again.

"You do realize how fucked this is?" Spidey this time,

as the man goes and lifts up his mask. He is neither "Roger" nor white teeth, but I relieve him of his weapon all the same; before either of them can re-raise theirs. I unload fast, a bullet for each, the Hulk quite nicely proving his own adage wrong. He was not in fact the strongest one there was.

No, that'd be me.

OF DREAM SCENARIOS AND PLANS

Maurice and me, we are men of extremes. Some would suggest different, stating over the top. Either way, the life we'd chosen to lead ensured we pretty much had to be something along these lines. Only when such traits spill over into things they shouldn't do complications arise for people like us. With this comes thoughts of over-compensation and I can understand why some people defer to this type of thinking. A misconception is what this becomes, as over-compensating and confidence are not much more than distant cousins once you've gotten under the hood. This comparison, it's what I'm attempting to enlighten Maurice to when the snake begins to twitch. Meant his eyes would no longer meet mine, and it's totally understandable why this occurs. I mean, the size of the thing Milligan hooked me up with is huge, taking three of us just to get it in the glass.

"You've always been big on fear, this we know." Nothing. Nadda. His concentration beyond me, through the glass and toward a situation which, for the time being, remained asleep. It slept because I'd tranqed the thing six hours prior, tranqing it hard, secretly hoping that today would become the day. "But do you recall telling me *your* greatest fear?" I know he didn't, not in the way he should, but this is the thing, the difference between employer and employees. Us guys, the workers, we don't forget. At least I don't. And when someone goes and lets you in on such a nugget, you go and squirrel that shit away. Never know when an opportunity may arise or a situation might present itself.

It's pragmatic is what it is; that and then some.

But I was getting ahead of myself. Realizing, I move forward, blocking Maurice's through-line to the glass. I hold up both my hands, flex what I'd been left with. "What I want you concentrating on is this. No, come on now, I want you to take a good hard look at the shit you set in motion. Used to be eight of these bad boys, right, but now you'd be hard pressed to say I have three. Used to have both ears too, Maurice, and this eye here, it never hung the way it does now. You think any of this is givin' you a clue as to the reason we are here today?"

I didn't require an answer, not really, and I tell the man so. "However, the place I do want to go is how we arrived here, as in our juncture. Translation being you should have maybe sent someone a little more inclined as to how one goes about one's job I think. Double translation, they should have at least gone and checked for a pulse before they buried me." Had his boys done that, I never get to show Maurice why I can no longer grow hair. The bullet that rode my skull from one temple to the next destroying the only part of my head I'd been able to comb since before the nineties.

"And you do realize how this makes you look? Not just for setting in motion what you did, but the reason as to why," I go on, saying my piece, Maurice looking more like an ugly Daddy Warbucks than ever before. "It looks to me like Janice never would have glanced my way if she were a woman being satisfied." His eyes expand at this, a little more rage let out of the box. Seems I'd gone and hit a soft spot. He double downs with snot bubbles, great big giant fuckers, which begin to foam above the gag. "You tryin' to tell me there's more than scrap metal in yer pants there, boss?" I smile as I say this, and I can only imagine the sight of me. Made me want to laugh and scream at the same fucking time. I mean, of all the things we'd done, all the jobs we'd pulled, that it would come down to a woman, a woman he'd already divorced...

Eighteen years gone in an instant, poof.

Laugh or scream. Shit or get off the pot. All told, I sometimes wish the grave had been a little less shallow.

"But what it comes down to, specifically, is how do you truly destroy a man? You obliterate that which he creates. Your words, Maurice. From your lips. Brings a whole new kind of light as to why I had junior join us here today." Perfection. All of it. Especially the veins upon his neck, each one now popping like cords. I go one step further and share what Milligan passed along. If I could see my way to rearranging a shoulder or two, my selection, it didn't much matter; python or anaconda, each would take a man. Done, it's on to constriction, the application, and how it's this which would come first.

What impressed me more is when I find out how the feet would go last, the anaconda going on like a condom, its meal taken by the head into a digestive system unlike any other. Truth be told, it kind of made me wish Maurice had had other children. Or that his child had children. And I know how this makes me sound. I do. But I also know how I feel.

"It's not like I had any kind of choice, Maurice. Not once I realized I was still alive." His nostrils flare at this, flare again, but I pull him forwards anyway, the legs of his chair screeching every inch of the way. Four feet from the glass, I plant myself beside him, my backside into the very same chair his son had been strapped to not minutes before. As I sit, my dream scenario continues. Maurice unable to do anything but stare, nothing but remorse leaking from his eyes. I acknowledge this by placing an arm around his shoulder and squeezing it with fingers both phantom and real. Twenty minutes on and junior's eyes flash open, his struggles against his bonds causing an agitation I'd been anticipating since awakening last fall. It brought a different type of panic to the festivities as well, and I respond first by standing, then by cutting the gag from Maurice's mouth.

I tell him I do this because I can. Because pragmatic or not, over the top or not, I was confident I was about to like what I heard.

AND NOW, BACK TO OUR PROGRAM

Until I realized she'd been fucking my husband the only thing my younger sister ever did to really piss me off was become a vegan.

"Don't stop on my account. I mean, it hasn't let you so far." Cheryl freezes, her naked body instantly tense. Michael's eyes fly open like blinds snapping to. He wants to say something, he does, and I can see as much, but for the moment he is gob-smacked. Good. I had their attention.

"You think I'm joking, just continue to stay as you are, Cheryl. I mean what I said: keep going. God knows it takes him long enough." I can tell she doesn't want to, not in the least, but I was as far from playing as I had ever been. To make this known I re-grip and inch closer, pushing both barrels harder into the back of her head. It does as I intend and in seconds she's back to as she was, taking my husband deep into her throat. "That's it. Show him how much better you are than me."

"Babe, please..." I don't know what made me angrier, that he called me babe or that he had spoken at all.

"I suggest shutting it, oh love of my life. Just lean

back and enjoy the show." Resigned, he complies and returns to how I found him, his neck propped up by two pillows against the mirrored headboard, his sister-in-law down home in his junk. All he could manage really, as his wrists and ankles could do nothing but remain as they were, each bound to a bedpost by a set of handcuffs I'm more than sure I'd purchased myself. His eyes were open now though, and quite possibly in more ways than one, but the fear I see in them is stuff which causes me to smile.

Not that I was enjoying myself. Well okay, maybe a little, and only because of what I'd planned.

I didn't always know, just suspected, and even then only because of the perfume I'd gotten Cheryl for Christmas. I'd catch little whiffs of it here and there. What pushes the idea further is this usually started at the beginning of the week, come Tuesday, which happened to be Michael's day off. The one blonde hair I found under my pillow though—this is what became the be-all-end-all. The rest is just simmering wet rage. The shotgun too, and what I was about to create, but that would just be described as aftermath, what I'm sure most of the world will refer to as white noise once everything's said and done. I'd get some notoriety, sure, but what it wouldn't do is get me what I wanted most: my life before it'd been turned to shit.

"That's it, Cheryl, take him slow, just how he likes. Heaven forbid he ever return the favor, though." She won't look me in the eye, not by way of the mirror, but she's trembling by now, my sister of forty years. For twenty-five of them she'd been vegan, as I've said. This pissed me off, as I've also said, but the type of red which accompanied that lifestyle change had been a different pill than this; the tint or shade more acceptable than the one reserved for intruding on another woman's marriage say. Funny how both these things involved meat though, isn't it? Not ha-ha funny, just…

"Christine?" And there is definite remorse in his voice. I didn't care, not anymore, but he didn't quite know that yet. Not if I knew my husband. "I can only apologize. We were wrong. Let's stop and we can talk about this…"

"Like adults? Pretty sure that's a road you don't want to venture down, Michael." His shoulders slump at that, as they have whenever he has never gotten his way. Then he begins what I call his "routine," which happens whenever he is close to climaxing. It makes me cringe, seeing it from this angle, but I bought and paid for such things long ago. Means I have no one to blame but myself. Well, not exactly. Not with both of them still in front of me.

"But you know what really kills me? And it's not only you two doing what you're doing. It is, don't get me wrong. But you, Cheryl. You're the one who pisses me off the most out of all this. Look at you, how you look. Any man could be yours. But no, not fucking good enough. Not for you. You choose to do this instead. You know what it reminds me of? Reminds me of when you went and told us you were done with meat. You remember that? Would have been fine if it only affected you, but it didn't, not back then. It meant *we* had to change for *you*. I lived with it. Mom and Dad lived with it. But we shouldn't have had to. It's because you're selfish, Cheryl, and because you always have to have things revolve around you. It's why the punishment that presented itself…I think it's the reason I found you two like this and not the other way round. You figure out what I'm going to make you do yet, Cheryl?" I can't say she knows, not with any degree of certainty, but the uncontrollable sobbing and shaking was enough for me to reposition the steel through the curls of her hair one last time.

"You're going to take it all. Not just to the base as you can. And you are going to use your teeth as you never have before. You are going to eat your meat, Cheryl, and you are going to like it." Her head begins to turn from side to side at this. I come forward again, the movement forcing more of my husband down into the cave of her throat. It pushes Michael past the point of no return but it does other things as well—things I had come to dream of. The first is the realization I see dawn in his eyes; that he now knows he is more fucked than he previously thought. Second is a stretch, as it wasn't my mouth upon him, but the odds of Michael coming just as a part of him was going had gone and entered the realm of possibilities. And third, well third I have always known—that self-preservation and selfishness are pretty much one and the same.

Meant she'd remember to chew before she swallowed.

TEN OFF THE TOP

As my mother grew older she sometimes shit herself she got so scared. Not many people knew this about Olivia Dunn, which isn't so hard a thing to believe. What is hard to believe is the way she left this world and the reason why. The why part involves me, or more so my problem, and if I had the choice I would certainly turn back time in an attempt to rectify this. Since I can't I'm stuck with what we'll call the lowest common denominator, which, if I'm truthful, is the whole reason things have played out as they have.

"And just because your daddy was some kinda war hero, it makes you no more special than the next guy. Mikey, you shoulda just paid." He was right of course, but it's not a particular point I choose to dwell upon. I had a problem, sure, and I owed some big goddamn bucks, but it was not like I wasn't ever going to pay. It was my timing which was off; that I felt mine was more important than theirs. Again, my fault, and I accept as much, but what they did to Mom. That's what keeps me up most nights. "Had you done this, nothing like this ever woulda transpired. Since it did, fine, we live with it. What I mean to say is I'll knock ten off the top for your trouble." His forehead creases as he says this, his big body coming forward as he laces his hands upon his desk. Smug, he motions to his goons on either side of me. They are brothers, Frank and Johnny P, and in an instant my face is introduced to tile floor. "What it doesn't mean," Sal continues. "Is that you don't get yours."

The beating is quick but ruthless, and by the time they're done my dominate hand is slightly lighter than how it arrived. And you know what? I took it. Truth be told, I would have taken it before they did what they did. But they didn't do that. They chose to go and use an alternate route to get my attention. I believe in this business they call it fair play. In mine it's evil with a capital fucking E. It's fine though, all good, as I am what my mother made me: a patient man. I'm also a gambling man, but that's neither here nor there, and it's not really something I wish to discuss, not if I can help it. Meant I might have to look in a mirror. Meant I might have to…

Where was I…

Oh yes, loose bowels always getting the better of Mom when she'd least expect. Frank and Johnny P are the reason for her final bout, the brothers I'm told only there to send a message. Inside, a different door opens, and the younger of the two, Johnny, is unable to reconcile the affliction he's walked into. Two punches later and it's me cleaning up what Johnny refused to smell. I knew it would happen sooner or later, my profession being what it is, but the manner in which she is delivered to me, this is what I cannot abide.

It wasn't punches that did my mother in.

Not after I get a look at what remained of her face.

Causes me to flashback to when the brothers put me to the floor in Sal's office. In hindsight I see Johnny's shoes as I saw them then, up close and personal, and then the sticky bits I hadn't noticed jump out at me, each of them screaming. They focus me, take on a different form, a deeper meaning, and it's at this exact point in my life that clarity does what clarity does best.

When it fucks me in the ass.

But my hands were tied. One man against a sea of many. So I watched instead. Then waited and healed and paid. I also continued to process loved ones here at the Dunn Funeral Home. The same thing I had been doing since before I turned owing twenty grand into forty and then doubling the number by not watching the time as I should have.

If I were a real man this is where I might choose to talk about the elephant in the room.

Since I'm not I will instead say it's four years until I am given any type of opportunity to achieve what I'd been looking for. And be it coincidence, irony, or however you fucking well describe fate, I still smile when I think of what has gotten me here.

"Very sorry for your loss." We're in the biggest of my visitation rooms, the place a zoo of people who looked as slick and somber as movies portray. He's greyer now, mostly around the sides, but it's his weight which speaks of all the good living he had going on. Taking the hand he had his men lighten in his, Sal goes overboard, adding his other one to atop the pile. Did he realize? Sure he did. It's what men like him lived for. In response I put my free hand on his shoulder and look him directly in the eye.

"Anything I can do, anything at all—do not hesitate to ask." As I hoped, he doesn't, and all of a sudden I'm making calls, ensuring it's his people who cater the funeral, his people who usher attendees in. In the process I give my own employees the day off, stating what most of them already knew: what Sal De Palma wants, Sal De Palma gets. Complete, it's on to the lady of the hour, Sal's mom, and the alterations her body would require. I do my best to be respectful but end of the day, wanted or not, I'm still inside part of a woman I had no right being inside of. Doing this brings my own mother to mind, and how could it not? But I had to push on; had to follow through. You know why right? I don't have to spell it out for you, do I?

So back to the hollowing out, back to the placing of devices. All told, I secure sixteen claymores to the inner perimeter of the casket, all obscured by an off-white frill ordered special just in case. Each mine sits as it should: FRONT TOWARD ENEMY. Beneath Sal's mom's blue pantsuit is a whole other story: fifteen "pineapple" grenades resting within the canal her son climbed out from. All ordnance courtesy of a life long past gone. My father's collection from a time I can't even begin to comprehend.

Set to go off once the pallbearers begin to lift, it will do as I intend, destroying an entire line of De Palmas as they sat and paid their respects. It will destroy my establishment too, and yes, I'm sure I will be caught. It doesn't matter though, not really. Not when one truly understands what they've become.

You're only given one mother in this life. Fucking cherish her.

NEVER ONE TO
DO THINGS BY HALF

He knows he's fucked the moment I ask if it should be Agent Brand I call him now or would it be better if we still went with Hank. I tell him I can't do Ryan though, a name I just couldn't comprehend when I looked at his face.

"Slide it over to Max and Jeffrey there. Good. Good. You gonna make me ask about the one in your ankle holster?"

I offer him a smile. Then I tell him *he* should smile, as he'd made it, now within the heart of where all the magic occurred. I concede our operation has been mobile in the past and more than not the reason we have always been one step ahead. What excited me more was what I was about to show him.

"Before I give you the grand tour, there's something I need to get off my chest." The method of his madness is what I wished to address. Not once had a person ever thought to come at us this way. Kudos is what I say to him, my appreciation as to how he posed as a doctor so great I'd decided to acknowledge this achievement with something I hoped he'd find just as clever.

Brings us to the cardigan I'm wearing. "Look familiar?" I hoped so. Jeffrey procuring it from Hank's own closet just this morning. "And what about how low I'm wearing this ball cap?" I go on and admit how I know it's the style Janet favors. Mention of the missus changes things, mainly the temperature of the room. Good. Meant I had his undivided attention. Still didn't stop me from telling him to drop the look. I mean, was I honestly supposed to believe he never once thought I might go this route if he went and got discovered? "You uphold the law. I circumvent it. It's the way this thing of ours is meant to work."

I move us forward, Max and Jeffrey bringing up the rear. Close to the end of our stroll Jeffrey moves up on past us and opens the blinds. I watch Hank, his eyes, but the man had become stone, would not give one mention as to how tight a ship I run, the view before us as clean and white and sterile as any operating room the world over. No matter. I was too encouraged. In front of us now the thing he wanted most. I direct his attention to the larger bins first. Retrofitted, they jut out from the walls on each side of each work station. To the left go legs. On the right, arms. The final bin sits in front, between each set of doors, and is what we refer to as the "and/or bin."

"And I know how smart you are, Hank. So from a business perspective you can see where I'm coming from. If you wanted to, we could jaw numbers all day long. But bottom line, you still would not believe the amount of raw material we chuck per annum." He won't look at me, only stares on straight ahead. I understand this. I can live with it. Flipping the equation and we arrive at what it creates. When something different is required, a new deterrent set.

I give him a few more seconds and then ask him if he'd narrowed down the Big Four my business made most of its profit from. He still says nothing, but I know he knows, so there really wasn't much of a point in me asking him to list them. Instead I lament about the head. How, try as I might, I am unable to create a demand for that particular ten pounds. Sure we get the odd request for a certain shade of blue for some guy's blind daughter, and hey, we will happily accommodate when able, but on the whole, no, heads have always been a dead-end investment.

Hence the and/or bin.

Made me wonder if I was being as clear as I thought I was. If Hank realized the implications of us talking as we were. "If it's Janet you're worried about, don't be. She will never see this warehouse and I give you my word she won't be going into any of those bins." I get nothing. Nadda. Zilch. So I tell him it won't be his men going in either, the ones from the surveillance van we took care of before lunch. Still nothing. Left me no choice but to hit the fast forward button. "You however, you I'm gonna let live."

And just like that, a response. Or at least a turn of the head and a look into my eyes. I take it as a sign, move closer, and put my arm around his shoulder. "What I need you to remember is it could have been your parents

NEVER ONE TO DO THINGS BY HALF

coming through those doors. Could have been your brother and his litter of kids as well. This is what I need you to recall when all this is said and done and you and your friends try and come at me again."

The doors open, big as well as small, and through fluorescent light come Daniel, Becka, and John. Takes me a moment but I remember to tell Hank how much I appreciate their names, that each one sounded solid and strong. I then embrace the cliché, but only after the first gurney to work station transfer is complete. Hank couldn't care less if this would be hurting me more than it hurt him though, and it's why I afford him his time upon the glass. His struggle affects me more than I thought it would, however, and I cut things short because of this.

Taking their cue, Max and Jeffrey step forward, continue on, and in an instant Hank and the glass have become the fastest of friends. I wet my lips, clear my throat, and make sure stubble rubs stubble as I speak into his ear. "You aren't alone in this, Hank. Not for a moment. Yes we may be on opposing sides, and yes we might always be, but take comfort in knowing this decision was one that did not come easy. After all, I'm a father too."

ANNIVERSARIES OF THE HEART

It weighs on my mind every second of every minute of every day. Obsession does not describe me though, not to an accurate degree. I am him now. He, unfortunately, me. The difference, the main difference, being our retaliations and how we've chosen to implement the pain.

"Your ribs are showing." I close the cell door and put the tray down atop the roughed-in toilet. The chains around his wrists rattle as he adjusts himself upon the mattress, his demeanor in an instant changing to what it always changes to once he realizes what's on top of the tray. Took some doing getting him here too, emotionally I mean, and it isn't until his right eye is removed that he comes to understand what I have always known. That I was capable of doing what he only ever paid his men to do.

It meant his need of solid food was no longer required.

It meant he would never again wear shoes.

"You don't start drinking more, you're only going to give me a reason to go in there and excavate." He'd respond if he could, more so in fact, but his tongue had been one of the first things to go, going early, pretty much at the beginning of what we'll call year one. It was joined by his left thumb and right nipple later that same year. All three combining to become the least of what Reggie deserved. Little could I know how difficult it would prove to keep things healthy, let alone infection free.

"Not that I'd be adverse to such a thing. Not at all. Inner, outer, you know it's all the same to me." He makes the noise in the back of his throat, the one he's come to use to beg. I respond by asking him if he recalls when it had been me who'd begged. He turns his head at this, lowers it, the concrete wall suddenly the most interesting thing in the room. The response is far from new, coming into play about the time his need to stand while urinating became obsolete. The old fashioned way could still be used, sure, but the dribble aspect it creates, it's what forces the desired effect. Year three is when this occurs. Along with his nose and left ear it coincides with what would have been Becka's sixteenth year.

Today is a different day altogether. Today, Daniel would have turned ten.

"Do you remember what you said to me as you had them brought in? When your goons were holding me to the glass? You said how much you appreciated their names and that each of them sounded strong. I remember this, Reggie. I have never been able to forget." I have gone down this road before. I probably would again. As ever, he only nods, but then again, I've never given him much of a choice, not since tracking him down.

Caught, I'd been posing as a surgeon in a body parts

ring when my own cover is blown. Forced to watch, Reggie whispers in my ear as my children are strapped to operating tables and ripped apart and then thrown into bins. The reason I'm left alive is meant to be viewed as a deterrent, for when me and the agency I work for decide to come at him again.

Reggie's words. His arrogance. Not mine.

But it took years for me to find him, long after Janet left and I'd resigned.

"My son, he would have hit double digits today. Means he would have been just out of diapers when you had him taken down." More mewling. More trying to push himself into a corner which would never relent. "Because of this, in honor of this, I believe it's time I let you choose." He stops at that, waits, then raises his one good eye to mine. On his face sits everything he wants, everything he needs. It just might finally end. The chance having come at last.

It hadn't though. And never would. Not after everything that'd been done. But it gives me what *I* require. What I will continue to take from Reggie until I no longer can.

It meant we'd just begun.

AN OLDER TYPE OF CARE

"I never thought it would end like this, Rider. Not with another man's dick down my throat."

It'd been years between now and the last time the detective and I had done our bit. Retired from the job, Batista had gone on his way, fishing and the life of a cabin-man his reward. Me, I continued on, but slower, finding rage could age just fine. It was a surprise, then, when the man up and made contact.

Liver spots covered him now, a flurry, and nothing like back in the day. His hair was gone too, all of it, save for the beard. If he asked me to, I'd have put him down. This how much I'd come to respect this man. I say this not only because of the monster which ate at him, but for the Alzheimer's as well.

It is said that God can show mercy. Taking in the machines and fluids Batista was hooked into, I say He has forgotten and died.

"This isn't an isolated case either, Rider. I've done my homework." I agreed with him, even before I started digging into it myself. What we shared, my family's demise, it does things to men like Batista and I, breeding a certain type of contempt for a particular type of man.

One step beyond is what allowed us to do the things most would not. I am not wrong in stating as much, not when innocents are involved.

It started at night, first with missing time and then with something more. The nurse's name had been Gish, Robert J. Six months removed from his last position in another rest home and here he was, in Batista's rest home, preying on men weaker than he. Tall and gaunt, Gish wore Buddy Holly frames above a blade-like nose. An Ichabod Crane-type, though in reverse, predator instead of prey.

"And you think he's doctoring the meds? That about the long and short of it?" It was rhetorical, really, what I was on about, but Batista looked as though he needed to let it out. Figured I was as good a target as any.

"You haven't changed, have you, Rider?" I couldn't and would never, and only because I picture them still— my mother and sister as alive in my heart today as the day my search began. Finding them as I did is what sealed the deal, showing me how broken our system truly was, their remains the last clean breath I'd ever come to take. "Not that I'd expected you to. And really, I can't even say why I'd entertained the idea, even now. Honestly, if the cancer doesn't get me first, I swear the Alzheimer's just might take away everything we've ever done." Same old Batista: heart on his sleeve. The shirt was older now, sure, and clearly near the end of the wash, but the man was still the closest thing I had to a friend, wanted or otherwise. I'd be good to remember as much.

Done, I told him I would do what he asked, that he'd had me the moment I picked up the phone. He smiled at that, there in his bed, his old man face for a moment close to the man I began this journey with. Pillows behind him, propping himself up, he growls one last thing, "Do me a favor? Before you do him, make sure the goddamn bastard bleeds some, will ya?" Not a problem, the night nurse an easier mark than I thought once I got him secured.

Piece of scum taped to a chair, I'd taken Gish to a place I'd kept, one of the smaller ones. Brought back old memories, did this, to a time when my arms were stronger than the tools I had come to lean upon.

"You know why you're here?" He did. His eyes telling me as much: silent but for staring me down. I told him anyway, listing every ailment of each senior he'd drugged and then forced himself into. Finished, he finds his balls, tells me to fuck myself, and that I couldn't have had it more wrong.

"They wanted me to," is what he says, his eyes big and wide, like holes. I wasn't buying. Not after everything I've seen; the crazy he was trying to produce as far from real as real could get. Wasn't until the gun came out that we got to the business of what he really was.

"No," he pleads. "Just please…not my face. Not my face! My mother, man!"

Okay. The face it was then.

Batista would understand.

NO OFFENSE TO MR. NEESON

Let's get this right out of the way: I am not a good man. Not by any stretch of the imagination. Of questionable origins some might say. What? You don't read comics? Too bad—your loss. But hold on. This big bloke here? The naked dude behind me? This is what things are really about. He look a bit familiar maybe? No? I'll up and elaborate then.

He's a pedophile, a facilitator, and all around nasty piece of cunt. We'll get back to him in a bit, I think. First I need to explain what this all entails. Plain and simple, a cease and desist order is what this is. My employers proving themselves a different kind of breed, that's for sure. Takes balls for someone of their standing to associate with someone of mine, let alone draw up a contract.

You see what I'm saying here?

That's right, shitbirds, I am one of you. Not exactly like you. No, as that would put us in some kind of kettle calling itself black territory, but a dirtbag all the same.

Not anymore though. Nope. Now it's the side of angels I'm on.

How does something like this happen you suppose?

Bank. How the fuck else? My employers having almost as much as you I'd reckon. Difference being they have no qualms in spending every penny in an attempt to take you down. This brings us back to tape-boy here, your second-in-command. It may surprise you I know this. It may not. Either way I couldn't give a shit. What it should suggest is that I have a particular set of skills. And yes. Yes. I know what you're thinking. But before you get all up in my face let me just say that not only would I eat Liam Neeson for breakfast but I would reheat that motherhumper for lunch. Hyperbole you say? A man given to tooting his own horn?

No offense to Mr. Neeson, as I am shorter, thinner, and balder than he, but fine, we return to Marcus then. See how I've popped out his eyes? How I really tunneled my way through? Really changes the shape of a person's face, doesn't it? Might be why you failed to recognize him at first. But ho, look at this! Look how the flame begins to lick at the skin of his legs. You also might be wondering why I started at the bottom instead of coating the man from the top. Valid point. It's because I'm far from done; why I have begun to put him out. And there's really no easy way to say this so I'm just gonna go and say it as best I can: diesel fuel.

See how it flows into the parts of his thighs which have yet to harden and close? Some kind of pretty is what that is. And look! Look how everything runs like tallow now, like goddamn soft serve. Collecting into hunks on the floor.

Leads me to wonder if you realize where we're headed.

'S'okay. I'll give you a hint.

It ends. All of it. Not tomorrow. Not later today. Right fucking now.

You do not touch nor film one more man, woman, or child in the ways that you have. I have addresses, you see. I have appointment dates. I even have little Christopher's ask to good ole St. Nick. And just so we're clear, do not feel special. You want to know why? Of course you do. Because it's not only Mr. Big-shot-I-can-do-anything-I-fucking-well-please I'm talking to here but all you pieces of shit.

My employers have the means, the money, but more importantly they have the wherewithal to see this through. Makes me wish I kinda met them sooner now I think about it. Since I didn't, we'll go this route. I dare all six thousand, five hundred twenty-six of you to ignore this, to just scoff and delete the fuck away. Actually, I implore you. We found you once. We'll find you again. And hey! Hey, would you look at that! As you've been listening to me explain the way things are the diesel fuel has gone and eaten right through the muscle of the man who helped bring us here today. And seriously, look at those femurs! I mean, Marcus, dude, you had to have worked out! Brings us to the last little bit of it, then. Now that you've seen what your futures' may hold. Only going to say it once so be a bunch of dears and do keep up.

Try me, fuckers. I'm a goddamn angel now.

ACKNOWLEDGMENTS

Yes, all these stories came leaking from my mind. That is not to say I was alone in making this collection happen. Quite a few people have been instrumental upon this journey. First I would like to thank all the good people who took a chance on me all those years ago and saw something in the things I write. This includes all the talented souls at Out of the Gutter Online, Ron Earl Phillips and his crew at Shotgun Honey, Gary Duncan over at Spelk Fiction, Ben John Smith at Horror Sleaze Trash, and Josh Goller at the Molotov Cocktail. I would also like to give a special shout out to Tom Pitts, he being the man who put me on the path. Last, but not the very last, are my sister and brother, Terri-Lynn and Shane. Over the years they have been my sounding board, my supporters, and my extra sets of eyes. My wife has been all these things as well, but has come to sleep with one eye open for reasons which could or could not be misconstrued. Finally, there is Down & Out Books. Top of the list being Eric and Christy Campbell, Lance Wright, and Eric Beetner. Thank you from the bottom of my heart you guys.

Thank you for taking the chance.

Oh, almost forgot one: you. The one holding this. As I've been known to say: never has handsome been so kind as to the person who reads to the end. See you when I see you. Peace.

Beau
March 10, 2017

PREVIOUS PUBLICATION CREDITS

Some of the stories in this collection have been previously published.

Bartleby Snopes: "Darnell (Waiting on the Day)"
Bending the Rules, edited by Alex Davis: "Toad Baseball"
Horror Sleaze Trash: "Meanwhile, Back at the Ranch"
Out of the Gutter: "Never One to Do Things by Half" and "Ten Off the Top"
Out of the Gutter Online: "Alma," "And Now, Back to the Program," "Fire in the Hole," "Front, Then Center," "A Full, Upright and Locked Position," "Heavy Lego," "I Remember. "#TheMediumIsTheMessage," "More Than They Could Know," "An Older Type of Care," "The Only Thing That Fits," "The Place Before the Place," and "Size Matters"
Sein Und Werden: "In Preparation"
Shotgun Honey: "Coffee, Tea, and Me" and "Knit One, Purl Two"
Spelk Fiction: "No Offense to Mr. Neeson," "Recompense," and "Regrets, I'm Thinkin' Yeah"
The Molotov Cocktail: "A Better Kind of Hate," "Gank," and "Loose Impediment"
Underground Voices: "Bobby Charles"

Beau Johnson lives in Canada with his wife and three boys. He has been published before, usually on the darker side of town. Such fine establishments might include Out of the Gutter Online, Spelk Fiction, Shotgun Honey and the Molotov Cocktail. Besides writing, Beau enjoys golfing, pushing off Boats and certain Giant Tigers.

OTHER TITLES FROM DOWN AND OUT BOOKS

See www.DownAndOutBooks.com for complete list

By J.L. Abramo
Chasing Charlie Chan
Circling the Runway
Brooklyn Justice
Coney Island Avenue

By Trey R. Barker
Exit Blood
Death is Not Forever
No Harder Prison

By Eric Beetner
Unloaded (editor)
Criminal Elements
Rumrunners
Leadfoot

By Eric Beetner
and Frank Zafiro
The Backlist
The Shortlist

By G.J. Brown
Falling

By Angel Luis Colón
No Happy Endings
Meat City on Fire (*)

By Shawn Corridan
and Gary Waid
Gitmo

By Frank De Blase
Pine Box for a Pin-Up
Busted Valentines
A Cougar's Kiss

By Les Edgerton
The Genuine, Imitation,
Plastic Kidnapping
Lagniappe
Just Like That (*)

By Danny Gardner
A Negro and an Ofay

By Jack Getze
Big Mojo
Big Shoes
The Black Kachina

By Richard Godwin
Wrong Crowd
Buffalo and Sour Mash
Crystal on Electric Acetate

By Jeffery Hess
Beachhead
Cold War Canoe Club

By Matt Hilton
Rules of Honor
The Lawless Kind
The Devil's Anvil
No Safe Place

By Lawrence Kelter
and Frank Zafiro
The Last Collar

By Lawrence Kelter
Back to Brooklyn
My Cousin Vinny (*)

(*)—Coming Soon

OTHER TITLES FROM DOWN AND OUT BOOKS

See www.DownAndOutBooks.com for complete list

By Jerry Kennealy
Screen Test
Polo's Long Shot (*)

By Dana King
Worst Enemies
Grind Joint
Resurrection Mall

By Ross Klavan, Tim O'Mara
and Charles Salzberg
Triple Shot

By S.W. Lauden
Crosswise
Crossed Bones

By Paul D. Marks and
Andrew McAleer (editor)
Coast to Coast vol. 1
Coast to Coast vol. 2

By Gerald O'Connor
The Origins of Benjamin Hackett

By Gary Phillips
The Perpetrators
Scoundrels (Editor)
Treacherous
3 the Hard Way

By Thomas Pluck
Bad Boy Boogie

By Tom Pitts
Hustle
American Static

By Robert J. Randisi
Upon My Soul
Souls of the Dead
Envy the Dead

By Charles Salzberg
Devil in the Hole
Swann's Last Song
Swann Dives In
Swann's Way Out

By Scott Loring Sanders
Shooting Creek and Other Stories

By Ryan Sayles
The Subtle Art of Brutality
Warpath
Let Me Put My Stories In You

By John Shepphird
The Shill
Kill the Shill
Beware the Shill

By James R. Tuck (editor)
Mama Tried vol. 1
Mama Tried vol. 2 (*)

By Lono Waiwaiole
Wiley's Lament
Wiley's Shuffle
Wiley's Refrain
Dark Paradise
Leon's Legacy

By Nathan Walpow
The Logan Triad

(*)—Coming Soon

Printed in Great Britain
by Amazon